THE PRINCIPALS

A Selection of recent titles from Severn House by Bill James

BETWEEN LIVES
DOUBLE JEOPARDY
MAKING STUFF UP
LETTERS FROM CARTHAGE
OFF-STREET PARKING
FULL OF MONEY
WORLD WAR TWO WILL NOT TAKE PLACE
NOOSE
SNATCHED
THE PRINCIPALS

The Harpur and Iles Series

VACUUM
UNDERCOVER
PLAY DEAD
DISCLOSURES
BLAZE AWAY
FIRST FIX YOUR ALIBI

THE PRINCIPALS

Bill James

This first world edition published 2016
in Great Britain and the USA by
SEVERN HOUSE PUBLISHERS LTD of
19 Cedar Road, Sutton, Surrey, England, SM2 5DA.
Trade paperback edition first published
in Great Britain and the USA 2016 by
SEVERN HOUSE PUBLISHERS LTD

British Library Cataloguing in Publication Data
A CIP catalogue record for this title is available from the British Library.

ISBN-13: 978-0-7278-8642-2 (cased)
ISBN-13: 978-1-84751-743-2 (trade paper)
ISBN-13: 978-1-78010-808-7 (e-book)

Typeset by Palimpsest Book Production Ltd.,
Falkirk, Stirlingshire, Scotland.

ONE

2014

Of course, Martin Moss realized there was bound to be a load of bitchy spite, top-notch rattiness and abiding malevolence about the statue idea. Hang on, hang on. Update. It *began* as about the statue idea – *a* statue idea, singular – but soon became about the *statues* idea, plural, two of them: binary, a term well-known in higher education. Moss thought the second proposed statue could be regarded in a sense as the baby of the first, by a kind of *in vivo* rather than *in vitro* fertilization: out of a living thing, not a test tube. Official minutes, e-mails and memos about the two projects came to be referred to as 'Statue One (L.C.)' and 'Statue Plus (V.T.)'. It was thought that to call the later scheme 'Statue Two' might be to confer on Statue One a hint of precedence – precedence not just time-wise but as to status. No way.

Moss could swiftly and simply describe the origins of the 'Statue One' concept. Those bracketed letters, 'L.C.' were the initials of Lawford Chote, former principal of Sedge University (founded 1885, motto 'Onward Friends Of Learning') during the period of cuts and stringent financial restraints on public sector spending by the third Thatcher Conservative government. Chote had resisted these restraints and cuts and defiantly continued on a programme for Sedge of expansion and expense and galloping debt. Onward friends of learning. He had apparently claimed somewhere that the word 'Positivism' was tattooed on a part of his body not obvious in day-to-day circumstances. He also claimed there'd been plenty of room for an exclamation mark after it, as suggested by the lady tattooist, but Chote had declined this saying it would imply that his positivism was something startlingly unusual, whereas he considered it routine; as natural to him and inevitable as breathing. But, owing to this inveterate free-spending and positivism, with or without an exclamation mark, Sedge in the late 1980s had drifted very, very close to bankruptcy, ruin, total extinction. Onward friends of learning, over the lemming cliff. Martin Moss didn't enjoy thinking about it even so long after.

Utterly against Lawford Chote's wishes, an emergency troop of auditors from the Department of Education and Science had moved in and ultimately, as a result of their findings, it was arranged for Chote to be removed eternally from post. Onward, Chote, to anywhere but here. Half a dozen Treasury people also came from London and assumed temporary control of the university's finances to stop the money troubles getting even worse, the debt vaster. Once some sort of stability had been secured, they would recommend the payment from state funds of a special and hefty salvation grant.

When Sedge seemed likely to die, Chote was described to Moss by a colleague in the English Department as 'the only man in the world who has single-handedly destroyed a university, a university more than a hundred years old and named after one of its revered and famed Victorian founders.' Chote came in for a fair whack of such vilification and abuse. His drinking, rudeness, half-baked witticisms and gobby, turbulent aggression didn't help his case much.

However, that was 1987. Today, Sedge thrived. Moss was still part of it. That one-off salvation grant, plus a government-driven reshaping of the university's management set-up had worked, and worked so successfully that Sedge might soon be invited to join the select clique of British universities known as the Russell Group, including Oxbridge. On account of this remarkable progress, some influential voices had begun to ask whether Dr Lawford Chote might have been a long-term visionary rather than a reckless, half-daft, giddy, blundering prodigal. Would Sedge be what it was now if Dr Chote hadn't given it a violent, perilous, necessary push-start? Had he shown admirable spirit, doggedness and bravery in standing up to Mrs Thatcher and her philistine, vandal cronies? Had his badger's arse roughness and loud contempt for his enemies been the only means available to oppose Rightist political attempts to curtail the spread of university opportunity for all young people regardless of class and/or low family income?

It wasn't as though he stood alone in trying to repulse Thatcherism. Oxford University refused by a plump majority to award her an honorary degree in civil law because of her attacks on research funding. This, despite the fact that she had been a chemistry undergraduate at Oxford as a young woman. And Martin Moss himself had wondered at the time whether Chote's objectives were right, but his ways of trying to reach them sadly clumsy and a turn-off.

So, anyhow, Sedge admirably, gloriously resurgent. And so, also, a statue proposal from the senate and high board and the education press amounted to something more than a formal impulse to commemorate a past chieftain. It was certainly that, yes, but the proposal contained, too, a notable element of apology, of admission that Lawford Chote might have been unfairly punished, even victimised. The statue would be a tangible symbol of regret and of the wish to compensate for timorous, short-sighted error; perhaps, in fact, a symbol of belated love.

Martin Moss still taught and researched at Sedge, but not many other participants in this 1987 crisis were still around: retired, dead, or gone away to other appointments. The contritional statue had to be a corporate matter. It was Sedge itself bringing a plea for forgiveness. As someone on the high board had said, if the statue had a caption plaque, it ought to read: 'They done you wrong, Lawf,' or however that came out in Latin. Leftist members of the present senate and high board – a fair number – cherished retrospective loathing for Margaret Thatcher – as they would have for Mussolini or Genghis Kahn – and were keen to deliver any insult and posthumous kick up the jacksy, such as the statue scheme. Moss wasn't sure about his own attitude yet.

But all this centred only on Statue One. In 1987 the city had two universities, each of them touched by the crisis. And it had two principals, each of them touched by the crisis: Dr Lawford Chote and Dr Victor Tane. Charter Mill and its campus lay a couple of miles away in grounds that still contained the carefully looked-after, historic watermill which had given the university its name. At Sedge, though, it was usually spoken of as 'the leisure centre,' not because the staff and students were lazy but because one of its degree courses was Hotel Management and Leisure Pursuits. Charter Mill had been created from a previous polytechnical college in the 1960s. It offered, as well as traditional university classes, a range of practical, vocational teaching aimed very specifically at preparing students for the careers market: Hotels and Leisure; Journalism; Hairdressing and Beautification; Pop Group Management; Organized Crime And Its Defeat; Secretarial Skills; Advertising; Pin-ball and Fruit Machine Design and Repair. Motto: 'Let Knowledge Be Honoured.'

Charter Mill had been regarded by many at Sedge as OK and, indeed, worthy, but not really what a university should be. Founders of one of the Oxford colleges in the thirteenth century would surely be surprised to discover that a university included a department of hairdressing and beautification. A university's commitment should be to learning for learning's own pure, magnificent sake, not to train students how to land and keep a job, except possibly for a medical or law degree. Chote and many of his Sedge colleagues saw Charter Mill as hopelessly banal, plodding and non-intellectual. It was much smaller than Sedge and, at the beginning of the boodle difficulties Chote had suggested a virtual takeover of Charter Mill. That didn't mean he thought Sedge would benefit by offering a course in hotel management and leisure pursuits, and so on. But he lusted after the mortgageable value of Charter's buildings, watermill and general real estate; and the extra per capita government grant that would arrive for Sedge's increased student numbers.

Victor Tane very competently and solvently led Charter Mill. He had responded swiftly and efficiently to the calls for economising. Charter Mill would be an unburdened asset if merged with Sedge. That's how Lawford Chote had calculated things. Naturally, he would remain as principal of the combined institutions, thanks to Sedge's seniority and distinguished roots. Victor Tane could, perhaps, be taken on as deputy, though without any assurance that he would succeed to the principalship when Chote retired. Although Tane had a First and a doctorate, both in classics, from Oxford, and had won several prizes for the composition of Latin verse there, Chote considered that none of this could adequately offset Tane's connection with journalism production, including tabloids, presumably, pin ball machinery, pop groups and raves.

A merger of the two institutions did in fact take place though not at all as Chote had envisaged. Soon after the government intervention, Charter Mill took over the tottering Sedge, rather than the reverse, and helped bring about its recovery. Victor Tane became principal of the new place and Lawford Chote was humanely phased out, with no impairment of his pension or requirement to pay back some of the cash he had blown. The city now had only one university. Tane agreed that it should maintain the name, Sedge, and the Charter Mill title was also phased out, though the antique watermill endured. Yes, the reconstituted Sedge had begun to do very nicely. Gratitude to Tane still flourished long after he and Chote had died. As a result came the strong, unyielding lobby from many sources in support of 'Statue Plus (V.T.).' That is, if there were to be statues at all. Would they be sculpted to stand alongside each other like happy equally deserving partners? Or might one of them be slightly the more prominent of the pair? In which fucking case fucking which?

TWO

1987

Back more than a quarter of a century, Martin was thinking about a possible second home in Florida while talking in celebratory, milestone fashion to a lecture room full of people about something else. In the front row Mrs Rowena Chote, the principal's wife, most likely well tanked-up for the occasion, had fallen into a sozzled, uncompromising sleep which required him to raise the volume of his words so they could be heard above the belligerent, intermittent snoring. This intermittent nature of it made things deeply more difficult. In the periods of silence, people could quite reasonably hope it had stopped for keeps and therefore she didn't need to be woken up by a shake or elbow-dig from someone beside her, right or left, or both. She'd remain asleep, perhaps, but, although this might be hurtful and off-putting to the speaker, mere sleeping was not pro-actively disruptive: the opposite.

The principal himself, naturally, had a front row seat, also, but several places away from her, and when the snoring was at its heartiest, noisiest and, seemingly, most entrenched, tried to signal with a hand and leg movement that she should be jabbed or ankle-clogged into consciousness. Then, however, the snoring would pause and those next to her obviously prayed, fingers crossed, that the pause was in fact more than a pause, a finale, making physical intervention by them unnecessary. Although Chote continued to gesture that due force should be used to bring her back fully and fully appreciative to the proceedings, she might resent the treatment and turn loud and very nasty. And the principal personally would possibly in retrospect regret and/or deny, having semaphored the order to intervene. Lawford Chote could be extremely unpredictable and contrary – and exceptionally dangerous. Some described him as 'driven', 'committed', and 'intensely focussed'; others said 'anarchic', 'foolhardy', 'egomaniac', self-contradictory'. There were marginally fewer plus comments about the principal around than minus. If he knew this it would not bother him, Moss thought. Chote would say that positive, thrustful leadership always brought out the sly, miserable, feeble, envious, nugatory backbiters. Their niggles proved he had things damn right. They feared change. Yet he believed that change as directed, powered, by him equated with progress. He regarded himself as the future; and, also, a quite satisfactory present. He would certainly be the only university head in Britain – or anywhere else, most probably – who put a metric tonne of contempt into his voice when he used the standard term for his professional colleagues, 'academics'. He made it sound like a disease, say, 'shingles' or 'piles'. Chote had thick, dark hair that gleamed under electric light, a strong, straight nose, broad neck and shoulders and generally powerful looking, stocky body.

One of Sedge University's traditions that the Principal had decided not to pulverize to date was the kind of inaugural address being given now by Martin Moss in Sedge's Quantum

Hall. Moss had recently been promoted to a chair, a professor-ship, in English and American Literature and it was the rule and practice that those raised to this rank should mark the step up with a discourse about some typical aspect of their work. A congratulatory dinner would follow for selected guests in the newly refurbished staff dining room.

Martin Moss's topic was: 'The redundant double-whammy for Sir Clifford in D.H. Lawrence's novel, *Lady Chatterley's Lover*'. Why, he vigorously asked, had Lawrence made the titled Clifford Chatterley unable to get it up and so oblige Connie, his wife, to go for sexual satisfaction from Mellors, the gamekeeper? Surely if Lawrence wanted to portray the upper classes, represented in Clifford, as emotionally narrow and null he should have shown Clifford as like that, not because he'd been paralysed from the waist down by a World War I wound, perhaps received in valorous circumstances, but because the males of his social class were actually born and brought up emotionally narrow and null. Lawrence wanted, as it were, to boot Cliff in the crutch twice, once for being an aristo, and once for being neutered. Did Clifford deserve this extra disability, Martin demanded, his tone fiercely aggrieved?

He pointed the audience towards another novel dealing with impotence but with virtually the opposite tone, though published only a couple of years before *Lady Chatterley's Lover.* This was Ernest Hemingway's *The Sun Also Rises,* renamed *Fiesta* in Britain. Jake Barnes, the hero of this tale, had been similarly incapacitated in the war, but was treated by Hemingway as a tragic, admirable figure, hopelessly in love with the shag-around Lady Brett Ashley. Moss said he would admit, though, that in the novel by British author Anthony Powell, *A Dance to the Music of Time,* failure in the bedroom by the clownish Ken Widmerpool is treated as part of his general, pathetic social ineptitude. Did American fiction have something to teach the Brits about sympathy and tolerance?

Moss had picked the book for his inaugural because, despite this objection, he liked it overall. It had been unsuccessfully prosecuted for obscenity in 1960 and this acquittal had brought a welcome boost to freedom of expression. Moss had asked a gentle, dreamy girl student in one of his Sedge seminars what she thought of the book. Her reply had been nicely balanced, he thought: 'I can take the fuck and the cunt but am not keen on the shit and the piss,' she'd said. It had seemed a pity she was too young to have offered her opinion at the trial.

In Quantum Hall, Rowena Chote had slumped slightly to the left, her head resting on the shoulder of the university Developments Director, one of the Principal's inner, inner team. The Developments Director didn't seem to mind providing this cushion but, because he knew the Principal so well – his bursts of crazed temper and unforgiving, serial hates – he would find nudging or forcibly jostling her too much. In any case, she had quietened again now. The refusal to act by those sitting near to his wife had probably angered Chote. He'd regard them as craven jerks. It wouldn't please Lawford to realize they must be afraid of him. He'd believe good leadership should enthuse and, yes, inspire, subordinates, not scare them, paralyse them.

Moss continued his address and for a while at the lectern was looking down and reading from his crib sheets. When he raised his head again and glanced towards Mrs Chote and the D.D. to check the current state of things, he felt amazed to see she had opened her eyes, righted herself on the chair, and was staring with vast animation and interest towards Moss. She muttered something and smiled; he experienced a kind of triumphalism. He had broken her deep doze, harvested her attention. How, though, for God's sake?

He had been reading to the audience more or less robotically from the script while his mind went off to calculate what his new salary would justify as a bank loan to buy the Florida property. Now, though, he paused and did a super speed-read of the preceding chunk or two of his notes. He'd been talking about *Lady Chatterley's Lover,* her husband, bodily ruined, and her search for, and discovery of, sexual fulfilment with the gamekeeper; 'not invariably via the dedicated route,' he'd added. And now he thought he could interpret the words she'd muttered a moment ago: 'not invariably via the dedicated route,' she'd repeated. The happy smile had followed. Moss's lecture went well after that.

The staff dining room and bar on the second floor were reached by a wide, curving, azure-blue carpeted staircase. This had been installed lately on the Principal's orders at big expense and despite protests in the senate about extravagance. Dr Chote had declared he wanted a university staircase fit to figure in the kind of university he was making this university into. Impressive staircases gave extra character to their surrounds. The more modest, workaday stairway that had been part of the original building was torn out, broken up and the bits dumped. Moss knew that the Principal considered this as brilliant symbolism: Sedge was on the way up and now had a staircase apt for this ascent. The Principal had also commissioned a revamp of the dining room and bar themselves. They were panelled now in oak and the tables and chairs were also oak. He had said that royalty would most likely visit Sedge in the future to witness directly its outstanding advance, so the décor and fittings should be in keeping.

Dr Chote bought the Developments Director and Martin aperitifs. The Principal, like his wife just now, was smiling. Quite often a smile from Chote could be taken as a genuine, temporary guarantee of friendship and safety. 'Martin,' he said, 'Roy and I were wowed, delighted, at the way you dealt with that situation in Quantum.'

'Absolutely,' Roy Gormand, the Developments Director said. 'Wowed. Delighted.'

'Decisive, tactful, delicate,' Chote said.

'Certainly,' Gormand said. 'Decisive.'

THREE

1987

'Look here, Martin, I'm always on the alert for people who will bring inventiveness, subtlety, clarity to what I call my "action group" – Roy, of course, and a few others whom I can trust to see matters as they should be seen, and who will work with me to bring added initiative, merit and distinction to Sedge.' Chote knew he did need people of that kidney, yet their yes-man qualities sometimes bored and irritated him. Sometimes, like tonight, for instance, sometimes did more than bore and irritate him: sickened him. Roy would at least not betray him, desert him, in any battle, though. And there would be battles.

But the kind of help he and others could offer was not very much because (a) they would approve anything as long as it came from him. And (b) people knew the cronies would approve anything as long as it came from him and therefore gave no weight and, or credence, to what came from them. Someone like this young – youngish – Moss would be different. Moss had vision and the striking ability to explain that vision to others. Moss saw that Cliff Chatterley had been treated very poorly by D.H. Lawrence. Roy Gormand would not be capable of such insight. Moss was someone who could phrase a delicate comment about Connie's and Mellors' shenanigans that could wake up and interest Rowena even when she was comatosed and three-quarters pissed. Martin Moss might be of clear-sighted, sensitive use to him.

Clearly Moss was someone with high skills as a communicator. Lawford considered this could be valuable in presenting very soon his case for the proud advancement of Sedge, despite that fucking obstructiveness of Thatcher and her cabinet. Chote felt very glad now that he had not followed an earlier impulse to wipe out the tradition of the new-prof lecture, although he rated some – most – of the twerps who qualified as pompous farts, and very obviously pompous farts when they performed. Not Marty Moss, however.

'Perhaps it's a fault of mine that I haven't given proper heed to your qualities before, Mart,' he told Moss. 'Tonight corrects that. Thank heaven, I say, for Lady Chatterley's acquired taste for rumpy pumpy. Yes, rumpy. We're going to undertake some very testing manoeuvres shortly, I think, Martin, and I believe Roy will agree.'

'Absolutely,' the Developments Director said.

'I know I can count on you for support and help, Martin.'

'Absolutely,' Gomand said. 'I'm sure.'

Lawford thought he'd take Martin Moss out to see Charter Mill. This would be creative principalship. Chote disliked imprecise, woolly talk about his aims for Sedge. If Moss saw the Charter Mill buildings, the old watermill itself, and the playing fields it would give a tangible, touchable form to the general noise about expansion of Sedge. Most of it could be seen from the road: no need to get out of the car. Lawford wouldn't want to be caught spying: some people at Charter would recognize him, including Tane. Awkward speculation about his visit might start. Charter was a couple of miles away from Sedge, but many universities had bits of their campus scattered around a city.

Of course, Marty Moss might already be familiar with the Charter Mill spread. He had lived in the city for almost a decade, first as a lecturer, then senior lecturer, then professor. But Moss would not have looked at Charter with the sort of purpose Chote wanted now: looked at, to be forthright, looked at it as prey; as a potential prize. He wanted Marty to understand – would help him to understand – that, certainly, Charter was fine in its own limited way, but that it would be much safer, more comfortable, more distinguished, if – when – absorbed by Sedge.

Chote would admit that Charter Mill had charm, despite the plainness of the modern architecture – if it could be called architecture – but, surely, Charter could not exist independently and alone in the present tough economic circumstances. Charter *needed* Sedge and it would be only an act of generosity and realism to offer Victor Tane a rescue deal and a lift up to the kind of status implicit in Sedge, natural to Sedge, inherited by Sedge. He thought Moss would see things in this fashion – again, intended to *help* him see things in this fashion – and Chote would be quite interested in Martin's positive response.

At the post inaugural dinner, Rowena Chote had been to tidy up and joined them now in the bar. 'Wonderful, Martin!' she said. 'That D.H. – so smart and comprehensive about sex, isn't he? No wonder Frieda ran off with him, dumping an academic, as it happens, but don't let this bother you, Marty. I love the story of Frieda on horseback calling out that it's *so* thrilling to have something splendidly powerful between her legs. And Lawrence tells her to stop it, she's been reading too many of his books! And then there's D.H.'s *The Virgin And The Gypsy* where Joe Boswell, the sexy traveller, remembers to tell the maidenly Yvette his name after he's been to bed with her, trying to warm her up, both naked, after a flood. Such finesse! Yes, *do* get me a drink, would you, please Lawford?'

FOUR

1987

Chote moved off to the bar to fetch his wife's bevy. Watching him, she found herself doing what she often found herself doing lately: she'd try to work out what someone like Marty Moss really made of Lawford and the Lawford regime. Of course, Moss would have to respond in agreeable style to Lawford's friendliness: he was the principal, had a lot of clout and knew how to use it, pro or con. Also, he could shout louder than most. He'd had plenty of practice.

She suspected that there were those in Sedge who considered he had grabbed and continued to grab too much influence. They saw him as an autocrat, and non-collegiate. Perhaps he was, a little. Autocrats could keep going, though. As long as they came up with improvements, gains, success; that blue carpet on the new, broad staircase did look fine.

However, universities were inclined to regard themselves as deeply democratic, their policies decided by committees and votes after civilised, thorough discussion: checks and balances. Lawford lacked affection for committees and votes, and especially for checks and balances. 'Stick them,' he'd bellow. 'Did Julius Caesar have to worry about fucking checks and balances?'

Moss, she reckoned, would be thirty-six or -seven. She thought the views of younger staff like Mart about Lawford's style of leadership could be important. Although Lawford might – did – see himself as the future, the *actual* Sedge future, the calendared days, weeks, months, years and decades, lay with Moss and his contemporaries. The Roy Gormands, nearing retirement, would go along with Lawford at least partly because they wanted a quiet, unstressful rundown of their careers. Why invite aggro so late in the day, so late in *their* day? This might not be the attitude of the Martys.

She regretted now having gin-kipped and probably snored an unmusical bar or two while he did his obligatory, functional spiel. It would be bad if he turned cold and hostile. She felt she ought to demonstrate fast that she'd heard more of his stuff than might be apparent. The shut-eye period could have indicated concentration, an escape from distractions, couldn't it? OK, the snoring, if there had been snoring, knocked this interpretation into the ditch, but it wasn't certain that she'd snored and, if she had . . . if she had she had, no getting around that now.

She tried to recall earlier passages of his lecture, before the jolly section that had roused her, because from then on she'd stayed alert and radiantly wakeful in case he had more of the same on offer. She dredged her brain. Was something said about a hilarious absurdity in the trial? Oh, yes, yes, she could just about remember this.

She turned to him. 'Mart, you mentioned that idiot prosecution lawyer who asked the jury in super dudgeon whether they would allow their servants to read this book. How many jury members would have servants? What was the lawyer afraid of – that one of the housemaids would get hotted-up by envy of Connie's sportif shags and jump the homeowner in the scullery?'

'Order,' Moss said. 'They were scared publication would be a step towards destruction of social order. It was published first in Florence and everyone knew how riotously sexual people around the Mediterranean were. Britain must not accept such a dodgy, subversive import. That was the prosecution's line.'

A middle-aged, dumpy, wheezy-voiced man with a mop of grey hair and a crimson bow tie on a black shirt joined them. He carried a glass of what looked to Rowena like apple juice. 'Greetings, Al,' Rowena said. Alan Norton-Hord was editor of the local morning paper, a graduate of Sedge, and chair of the Former Students' Society. He'd occasionally turn up at a public performance like Mart's inaugural. 'We were just discussing order,' Rowena said.

'There can come times when order will mean repression, wouldn't you say so, Al?' Chote asked. He'd returned with her drink.

'The world has to be run,' Norton-Hord replied.

'Roy, what's your view?' Chote said.

'Oh absolutely,' Gorman said.

'Martin?' the principal said.

'An American poet speaks of the "rage for order",' Martin said.

'Wallace Stevens,' Rowena said.

'A possible evil,' Chote replied. 'It can be used to suppress and make us downtrodden, subservient. We must resist, mustn't we, Roy?'

'Unquestionably,' Gorman said.

This was Lawford's gospel. Rowena watched Mart's face but she couldn't read much reaction there. She thought that if Lawford prevailed, the blue stair carpet would be trodden on, but not by people who were downtrodden.

'Talking of resistance, how are things between you and the Universities Finance Centre, Lawford?' Norton-Hord asked.

Rowena switched her attention from Moss to him. His paper was one of a string run by the Roudhouse Gate company, including two national dailies. Now and then rumours, tips, facts possibly drifted down from London to Al Norton-Hord. Rowena wondered whether he'd decided to come tonight with Mart's lecture as a pretext; but in fact looking for a chance to get an unofficial chat with Lawford. A literature prof's prescribed palaver wouldn't rate as news.

'The U.F.C. and us?' Chote said. 'All serene as far as I know.'

'No . . . no signals?' Norton-Hord said. 'Intimations?'

'Signals as to what?' Chote asked. 'Do you know of any signals, Roy?'

'Signals?' Gorman said. 'Not that have come my way, I can assure you.'

'Apropos the cuts, the Thatcher cuts policy,' Al said.

'We don't engage in that policy,' Chote replied.

'This is what I mean,' Norton-Hord said.

'*What* do you mean, Al?' Chote said.

Rowena thought his voice might be on the rise.

'We have a university to run,' Chote said. 'We have bright new professors to appoint, haven't we, Mart?'

'You're kind,' Moss replied.

'Some irritation at the U.F.C.?' Norton-Hord said. 'I gather they've already had to deal with a similar situation in Wales – one of the Cardiff principals there being very resistant and bolshy.'

'What happens in Wales is hardly relevant to Sedge,' Chote said.

'Hardly, indeed,' Gorman said.

'Irritation at a seeming failure to comply,' Norton-Hord said.

'Comply with what?' Chote asked.

'Economising. Cutbacks,' Al said.

Lawford stuck his head forward over his glass of ale. He seemed to have decided against shouts, but did a snarl instead. He looked as though he was about to tear off Norton-Hord's bow tie. 'I'm not in the complying vein,' he said. 'Universities do not reach excellence by compliance, by kow-towing to political instructions. Some instructions, some orders are, as I've said, retrograde, defeatist, evil. Torch them.'

'We're being instructed, ordered, to go into dinner, I think,' Rowena said.

FIVE

2014

The emblematic blue carpet on the stairs to the staff bar and dining room was well over twenty-five years old now. In one or two spots the colour had faded a little and here and there were small, faint traces of intractable staining where someone might have brought in oil on her or his shoes from the car park. But overall it still did what Lawford Chote had required it to do in his spend and spend-again epoch: chime with the qualities of the high-grade university that he had sought to create from the Sedge of his days. The university had, in fact, moved up a fair way towards this glittering status, though not everyone would credit Chote and the hotel-standard carpet for providing lift-off. True, the number tending to think reasonably well of Chote had begun to rise, but it was from a very low start. Sedge had not yet produced a Nobel prize winner to scale the Chote stairway en route to a celebratory bucket of Taittinger. Perhaps very soon, though.

But Lawford Chote wouldn't hear about it. He died within a year of his readily assisted departure from the principalship. The arguments about his influence, worth, strategy continued. Martin Moss, chairman of the recently formed Commemorative Statues Committee had to find a way around these prejudices, doctrinal loyalties and antagonisms and produce a suitably agreed commission for the two sculptures, which could be presented to the senate and then, ultimately, to the high board for ratification.

A couple of times he had dreamt of Chote in full, scarlet trimmed PhD garb, but worn with heavy mountaineering boots, standing halfway up the blue-carpeted staircase, eyes challenging, dauntless, ablaze, and pointing with stretched out, stiff arm to somewhere even further up. Moss had the notion that this somewhere wasn't merely the staff eatery. In fact, on Chote's back, over the PhD costume, was strapped a cheap looking canvas knapsack which might well contain sandwiches and other refreshments for a journey, making the dining room redundant. No, Chote's commanding gesture in the dream urged staff towards brilliant, soaring, stratospheric Sedge achievement, perhaps that longed-for Nobel; or, taking into account Chote's ferocious ambitions for Sedge, the second or third Nobel, plus half a dozen memberships of the Royal Society.

Chote had been a decorated bomber pilot during the Second World War, and perhaps he had brought to Sedge something of the Royal Air Force motto, 'Per Ardua Ad Astra', meaning: 'By hard work we'll reach the stars.' Also, Moss recalled reading that when a member of the Black Panther racial equality agitators in the United States was asked by a would-be placator, 'Well, what do you want?' he had answered, 'Everything.' Lawford Chote had wanted everything for Sedge. Post mortem some of it had been secured.

'Height is going to be a problem,' Angela Drape (Environmental Engineering) said, her voice big, accustomed to reaching the back of a lecture room. It was the second meeting of the Commemorative Statues Committee. Several departments had been asked to supply one of their staff for the C.S.C. 'There aren't any actual measurements available as far as I know, but judging from photographs I'd say Victor Tane must have been at least six foot four, as against Chote's five foot eight or even five foot seven.'

'A problem in which way?' Bill Davey (French) asked.

'If they're put alongside each other to suggest equality of achievement – and this, surely, is how it has to be – in such proximity Victor Tane is going to dwarf Chote, make him look like a ballboy,' Angela replied. 'This is hardly the theme we're seeking to display in the two images. The very opposite.'

'We can't have Chote standing on a box to make up the difference, the way they did for Alan Ladd in his movies,' Claud Nelmes (Physics) said. Nelmes liked a joke, a joke always delivered deadpan; and, because most of his jokes were feeble, hardly jokes at all, many people didn't get that what he'd said was one: dead-and-buried-pan.

'But some statues have a plinth,' Bill Davey said. 'Chote could be jacked up a bit on one of those. Watching *Antiques Roadshow* not long ago I saw a statue of the boy David taking aim with his catapult to do Goliath and the kid definitely had a plinth. I got the idea he needed that plinth as much as he needed the catapult.'

'Surely most statues have plinths,' Lucy Lane (History) said, putting her nose-picking on hold while she spoke. 'Perhaps all. If Chote gets a plinth it would be an obvious requirement for Tane to get one, too. In any case, if he didn't have a plinth what would Tane's legs and feet actually be standing on? Indeed, plinthless, would Tane be able to stand at all? The point about plinths is that the subject's feet are of a piece with the plinth. Clearly, the feet are not feet in our usual day-to-day meaning of feet and capable of making a platform for their owner, enabling him or her to participate in cross-country or relay sprint races. Neither of the statues will be taking part in that kind of activity, though they were both highly competitive beings! These feet *represent* feet but are, in reality, shaped stone and of the same chunk of stone as is the plinth. This is the essential. Sculpted feet have no separate existence from the stone plinth on which the feet appear to rest, but do not rest in our normal use of that word, because the feet and the stone plinth are integral.'

'Those feet are not made for walking, regardless of the old song,' Davey said.

'I think we have to concede that both statues will require plinths,' Angela Drape boomed. 'Different size plinths would put us back to the same quandary as arises from the variation in height between Tane and Chote. A larger plinth for Chote would be seen as a sort of pitying aid to someone rather stunted. I can envisage the Chote statue coming to be dubbed among undergraduates "Principal Plinth".'

'We need to consider whether the statues have to be painstakingly, rigidly accurate as to height,' Wayne Ollam (Philosophy) said. 'Are we bound to reproduce their physiques exactly as in life?'

'We would possibly need to take advice from the sculptor on this,' Mart Moss said. 'Perspective, scale, contextual background are matters for a professional, I believe.'

'As Lucy very validly pointed out with regard to feet, these sculptures will be *representations* of the two subjects,' Ollam replied ruminatively. 'Likenesses. They will not have blood or bones. So, if they are to dispense with those human properties, are we obliged to try for strict accuracy as to tallness, shortness, fatness, thinness? Why this selective scrupulousness? Where is consistency? The great sculptors might be able to *suggest* blood and bones behind the surface of their work, but it is *only* a suggestion.' Ollam's way with emphases was mild but effective, Mart thought – perhaps *more* effective because the listener would not feel button-holed, bullied and brayed at, and therefore resistant to the message.

'The spectator *infers* the blood and bones but this inference is a tribute to the sculptor's skills; and if there is no spectator – say when a gallery has closed for the night – if there is no spectator to infer the living innards then that statue has no innards. It is stone, end of story. I know some sculptors claim that the finished, statued figure is actually implicit and detectable by them in the block of stone when it is *just* a block of stone. Arty bullshit, I'm afraid.

'Consider Rodin's *Le Penseur, The Thinker.* This is a man seated, sort of crouched forward, his hand up to his chin, as if he's giving some topic a hell of a lot of concentration. But notice that "as if". We – the viewers – have to imagine the statue's brain must be really whirling. We can't *see* his brain, though. We have to take his brain on trust. What we're looking at is a lump of bronze – not stone now – bronze that Rodin has worked on with his chisel so as to make us say, "If this were somebody real he'd obviously be trying to work something out in his head, truly cogitating in an unhurried, plodding fashion." We don't get *into* that head. We have to help Rodin by picking up the hints and doing a deduction from them. We are dragooned by our culture and by habit to supply what Rodin can't – the "thinks" of the thinker. What I'm saying is that statues of their nature, yes *of their nature,* cannot give a full, as it were, account of the person they are meant to resemble and therefore, by extension, the physical appearance of the statue need not be slavishly, pedantically focussed on such banal, virtually random matters as height, girth, general build.'

Elvira Barton (Classics) said, 'I would put this in terms of a syllogism, the medieval style of debate where there are certain assumptions which may be or may not be accepted by both sides; and a conclusion that is deemed valid or invalid. It's like this: all statues are essentially lifeless; lifelessness is clearly not a characteristic of life; therefore, no statue need embody every aspect of the person featured in the statue whether still alive or having been alive.'

'But if Lawford Chote had been a dwarf it would surely be ridiculous not to recognize this in his statue,' Jed Laver (Industrial Relations) said. 'People who remembered him when alive would inevitably have his dwarfdom in mind as one of his most headline characteristics. I do not mean in any respect to mock or malign dwarfs but their stature is bound to be a distinguishing factor. Acquaintances, relatives, friends, even enemies, would definitely feel there was something wrong about the statue if it ignored that basic element. After all, the dwarfdom might have psychological implications – inner resentment that he should fall into this category; perhaps a special vigour and defiance in an understandable attempt to assert he can deal with any problem as efficiently as taller folk can.'

'Why do you pick on Lawford Chote for this unpleasant fantasising?' Gordon Upp (Linguistics) asked.

'No intention at all to denigrate Chote in any way, Gordon,' Jed replied. 'I could just as easily have used Victor Tane's name, though dwarfdom for somebody well over six feet is perhaps more difficult to reconcile, even in a make-believe narrative.'

'And you *didn't* fucking well pick Victor Tane, did you? You reserved your vicious, bilious meanderings for Lawford.'

Martin Moss said, 'I feel we have had a very productive early stage meeting. Certain boundaries and central objectives have been identified and positively, promisingly, touched on. This will set us up very well for our next scheduled session in a fortnight. I have no doubt some informal private discussions will take place in the interim between committee members and we should all return ready to take matters in this supremely worthwhile project a further distance forward.'

SIX

1987

'**D**o I understand him right, Mart?'

'Who?' Moss said.

'Al Norton-Hord,' Rowena Chote said. 'About the signals, or no signals, from the Universities Finance Centre. What did the signals say, if there *were* signals?'

'I'm not sure I understood that myself,' Moss said. The dinner following his inaugural had ended and people were dispersing. Rowena Chote had made her way to him, as if to offer a handshake and hug in final congratulation; but he realized now mainly to quiz him about what the journalist had said. Norton-Hord had already left.

Mrs Chote would be in her late forties. She had a broad, friendly face, alert blue-grey eyes, perhaps refreshed by the lecture room snooze. Mart had been in company with her before and knew she had a big, loud laugh, but only when she found something genuinely funny, not just an attempt to break the ice or indicate a disarming, sociable nature. She wore a blue, two-button wool jacket over a lattice topped white blouse, and blue long-panelled skirt. Her hair was assisted fair-blonde worn at shoulder length. She had a snub, small nose, but, as they all knew now, obviously capable of that noisy, disproportionate snore din; yet also to sniff subconsciously that it was time to wake up and hear some stuff about interesting sex.

'And the comparison with a similar situation in Wales,' she said. 'What situation?'

'Expenditure outstripping income, I imagine. It's happening to most universities to a major or minor degree because of government cutbacks, even Oxbridge,' Moss said.

'And here, at Sedge, it's a *major* crisis, is it?'

'I don't think Norton-Hord said a crisis, did he?'

'No, his tone said crisis, though,' she answered. 'He spoke of signals and the U.F.C.'s possible irritation with Sedge, and presumably with Lawford.'

'It wasn't clear where his information came from. But *was* there information at all, or just a volley of questions?'

'He's a journalist. Most of their information comes from other journalists, doesn't it? Sometimes it's right, all the same. It's how Lawford seemed to take it, wouldn't you say? The signals, the irritation. That's what they appeared to mean to him. Suggestions of trouble – of crisis, yes. He was rattled. We came very near to one of his famous in-depth, state-of-the-nation, rages. I called time – and only just in time.'

'The move into dinner?'

'I have to look after him, Mart. He'll sail daft and determined towards heavy weather. In some ways it's admirable, loveable in him. Courageous. Defiant. But also obsessive, egotistic, vain, suicidal?'

'He does stir up the adjectives.'

'I hope you will help me with this. He's got a good cause, higher learning for anyone who wants it, and thinks this such an obvious boon that as long as he doesn't waver it's bound to convince others and win through. This is a mission with him, a holy grail job. But it isn't bound to. He could get mangled. We must have some *real politik*. My speciality, but I need help with it.'

This made two of them – Mrs Chote and Chote himself – asking for Martin's assistance. He hadn't known that literature professorships at Sedge came with so much baggage. As Mrs Chote had said, Lawford Chote did have a good cause and Moss would back it. But, as she'd also said, not everyone admired this objective, and some of those who didn't were powerful and clever and ruthless and intent on hacking away at public spending, university public spending in particular.

Mart was out for a spin in Chote's office Volvo, the principal driving. He'd asked Martin to come for an excursion with him and take a look at Charter Mill. The invitation had seemed to Moss loaded with a kind of special excitement, perhaps touched by some of that obsessiveness Rowena had mentioned as strong in Lawford. Moss felt it was as if Chote believed the sight of the Charter layout – the actuality of it: brickwork, cement, windows, doors, footpaths, the 'Charter Mill University' name board, gold lettering on black – yes, these undeniable proofs of brazenly being there, would help show Mart that a change was required, urgently required.

Maybe Chote remembered an episode in Boswell's *The Life of Samuel Johnson* where they were discussing Bishop Berkeley's theory of the non-existence of matter. Boswell declares it's hard to refute this. In response, Johnson gives a large stone a hard kick and says this is how he refutes it. Did Chote want to show Mart the reality of Charter Mill and so persuade him that in the present tight national economic circumstances, Charter should be part of Sedge, and part of Sedge soon, for its own good as well as for wider reasons? Chote might believe that almost anyone would be convinced of this, but especially somebody as enthusiastic about higher education as a new, go-ahead, perceptive prof who had detected unconventional hetero-bonking in *Lady Chatterley's Lover* and knew how to talk about it with delicate tact.

'There's much that's admirable about Charter, I would never

deny it, Mart, but what's an imperative now is for it to be
brought to full fruition. This simple move will benefit everyone.
When I consider Charter, I imagine how the great landscaper
of the eighteenth-century, Lancelot Brown, might have reacted
to it: "This bog-standard little lot has capabilities." The watermill? Of course, living locally, you'll have seen it before today.
It has charm. Gimmicky? Yes, but I'd be willing to keep it in
place for a year or two. There'd be no real point after that,
would there, when the name and identity of "Charter Mill" have
been expunged? I don't mind an occasional slip into sentimentality as long as it's *only* occasional.'

Chote was silent for a while, as they drew close to Charter.
'They're putting a gaggle of auditors into Sedge, you know, Martin.'

'Who?'

'Universities Finance Centre, alias the fucking philistine,
fascist government.'

'Is that what Norton-Hord was talking about?'

'Of course, they'll come looking for faults and trying to slant
things that way,' Chote replied. 'They'll have been briefed – i.e.,
brainwashed. These people live with figures and know how to
cook them to suit whatever the doctrinaire politicos want. Will
they get anywhere near understanding the Sedge-Charter
Mill situation?'

'The situation in which sense?'

'The sense that unification, merger, takeover – whatever term
we use for it – such benign unification will see the end of any
difficulties Sedge might have, or any that Charter Mill might
have, too. They should realize – should be helped to realize –
that the solution to any troublesome circumstances is right there
in front of them, plain and guaranteed. If Norton-Hord comes
to you for insights on things between Sedge and the U.F.C. it
would be best to explain matters to him along those lines, Mart.
He's a reasonable bloke. I got somewhat ratty with him the
other evening, but he knows that's only the unmalicious knock-
about of debate. Healthy. Challenging. Honest.'

But he more or less snarled these terms. He probably despised
their comfy, prim harmlessness. 'OK, the Charter Mill property
is functional bordering on hideous, and many of the courses
offered there are somewhere between workaday and farcical,

but I'm willing to take them on, the whole package, Mart. It's necessary for the eventual good. It would be dereliction on my part if I didn't seek to organize rescue.'

Moss felt uneasy. Was he being sucked into croneydom, as others, like Roy Gormand, had been? Did the share-my-pilgrimage-out-to-Charter edict show a wish by Lawford to bring Moss into his select, inner cabinet? It was as though Chote had said, 'Come join with me in sizing up a piece of real estate that we – you, I and others akin to you – will benignly grab for our portfolio, acting out of generous kindness to the Victor Tane combo. And, if you should be talking to Norton-Hord, talk to him as I recommend you talk to him and not as you might have talked to him if I hadn't had a word with you, Mart, about how to talk to him.'

In general, Moss saw the reason for Chote's colonising campaign and thought it right. Some of the detail troubled him, though. Martin knew that no grand, mystical experience would take a hold on him as they ogled Charter Mill. And if that had been what Lawford wanted for Moss, he had failed.

SEVEN

2014

'**P**roximity,' Lucy Lane said, her thin face taut with triumph, as though hooking and landing this notion had been a fearsome struggle but, now, here it was, conclusively ashore. 'Have we properly considered whether proximity is essential?' Using a tartan-themed handkerchief, she wiped one of her fingers. This cleansing job went on for more than a minute while she tried to dislodge one super-sticky bit of nose debris from under her index nail.

'Proximity in which regard?' Bill Davey asked. The Commemorative Statues Committee (C.S.C.) was in session again, Mart Moss chairing, as before.

'Are we assuming, without due thought and analysis, that

Lawford Chote and Victor Tane – the statues of, I mean, obviously – are we assuming that Lawford Chote and Victor Tane, or to reverse this for impartiality's sake, Victor Tane and Lawford Chote, have to be placed close to each other? What I meant by "proximity". It is this envisaged proximity, isn't it, that gives rise to the height problem? Proximity will invite comparisons; no, will *enforce* comparisons, in fact. Someone short alongside someone tall, or to reverse it, someone tall alongside someone short, is bound to be noticeable. I recall that television sketch about social class, with the tallest man on the left representing the upper class, someone not quite as tall representing the middle class, and someone short representing the lower class. The differences in status are quickly made graphic by these, as it were, symbols. Something similar might occur in people's reactions to the two statues if they are, so to speak, cheek by academic jowl.'

'And yet some might think of the Book of Amos, chapter 3, verse 3,' Elvira said.

'Might they?' Lucy said.

'"Can two walk together except they be agreed?",' Elvira replied. 'This is what's known as a rhetorical question, being, in truth, no question at all because the answer "No" is built-in. The Bible is fond of rhetoricals. Probably the first is, "Am I my brother's keeper", Cain requiring an "Of course not" from God?'

'True,' Angela said.

'Putting me in mind of the three-legged race at school,' Gordon Upp said. 'A pair of contestants have their right and left legs tied together and they must not simply walk but run as a unit, so they certainly need to agree about how to do it or they're liable to pull each other over. Same with coalition governments: some progress possible, but, also, some bad difficulties.'

'At least one statue would have to be parked outside the main building, surely,' Bill Davey said. 'A valuable identifying marker to the people passing in the street, some of whom will not be familiar with the city. The caption plate would give the appropriate name and then, "Principal of Sedge University" and his dates.'

'"Main" is rather a loaded term, isn't it?' Wayne Ollam replied. 'This is, indeed, a university. That title doesn't come without deep implications: all its buildings are of *universal* significance. If we speak of a "main" building we speak also by irresistible implication of a "main" statue and of another building that is not "main", is less than main. This is to cave in to the kind of ranking of the two principals that I think it's accepted we should skirt.'

'If the statues were sited on separate campuses, which I take to be the hinted suggestion by Lucy, taking into account her down on proximity, there wouldn't seem to be much doubt about what Bill calls the "main" part of the university – its proper designation "Humanities" – and the other out at what was Charter Mill, now re-christened as "Life Sciences",' Upp said.

Lucy asked, 'Why do you say—?'

'I know what you're going to query,' Upp cut in.

'What?' Lucy said.

'Why do I say "out" at Charter Mill?' Upp answered. 'What constitutes its "outness"? I was very aware, believe me, of the provocative nature of the word. Yet there is some truth involved, is there not? The Life Sciences block *is* out, in the sense that it's out on the edge of the city, not central, as is Sedge. The watermill has been removed, yes, so that further student accommodation could be constructed on that spot, but there is still something bucolic, something agricultural – perhaps pleasantly bucolic and agricultural, comfortingly rural – about that area. However, if one of the statues were consigned to there, malicious folk might see in it something yokel-like, no matter which of the principals it might be: village idiots could be short or tall.'

'"Consigned"?' Lucy said.

'Freighted,' Upp said.

'If a plurality of statue locations *were* preferred,' Elvira said, 'it would almost certainly mean the Tane figure must go to that erstwhile Charter Mill, now Life Sciences, spread.'

'Why do you say so?' Jed replied. 'Why?'

'This was Tane's home ground,' Elvira said.

'Yes, it *was* his home ground, but he could play away,' Jed replied. 'He very evidently did not remain restricted to that home ground. In due course he was able to make both campuses his home grounds, in fact.'

'He did "bestride the narrow world like a Colossus",' Wayne Ollam said.

'That is why Sedge still exists and comprises the two components; and why we are undertaking these discussions on the duality of statues,' Jed said.

'There's a C.P. Snow novel based on an actual situation called *The Masters*,' Elvira replied, 'about the election of a new head at a Cambridge college – in reality, Christ's. I feel if anyone were writing a tale about *our* proceedings it should be titled *The Principals*.'

'It would be inaccurate, misconceived, unjust, wouldn't it, to send Tane "out" – if I might take Gordon's word for a moment – out to this far-flung region?' Jed said. 'I think of Napoleon being transported to St Helena. I think of the leper forced to take himself off to the wilderness.'

'Well, that's fucking ludicrous,' Upp replied.

'Would you want the Chote statue, instead, put at Charter, now Life Sciences. Jed?' Lucy asked.

'I'm saying only that it would be an error to ship Tane there, merely on account of his earlier connection,' Jed said.

'Wasn't there some rumour about Tane needing to use staff from the Organized Crime And Its Defeat department at Charter Mill to protect himself when the 1987 situation was at its worst?' Theo Bastrolle (Business Studies) asked. It was the first time he'd spoken at any of the C.S.C. meetings. Mart came to think that Theo often seemed to follow a personal brand of thoughts, not much related to any of the other comments and debates.

'Yes, I heard something along those lines,' Davey said.

'Occasionally, I feel we are ignoring one of the chief sources of information potentially available to us,' Lucy said.

'Oh, which?' Upp said.

'Can I be alone in thinking this?' Lucy said.

'Which?' Upp said.

'Martin,' Lucy replied. 'Our chair. I realize he has to avoid bias in this role, but perhaps that shouldn't prevent him offering some neutral, informal guidance. After all, he has the kind of first-hand experience of the period which most of us lack. I have in mind extra light on the two principals' characters, which might help us with the physical style – styles – we recommend for the statues. For instance, I was away in Cardiff a little while ago and in the shopping centre saw a statue of the great Welsh politician, Aneurin Bevan, and the sculptor had managed to get the impish, belligerent forward crouch I'm told Bevan would adopt when making one of his fierce speeches. I'll have a trawl through the Sedge and Charter archives looking for material that might be useful in this regard. It's quite common knowledge, isn't it, Mart, that you and Lawford Chote were buddies during the crisis months? Nothing reprehensible or even surprising about that. But it could be relevant. I'm not suggesting cronyism, though I expect there *was* some of that: it's endemic in any organisation.'

'Certainly,' Elvira said. 'The disciples.'

Moss said, 'He chaired the panel that appointed me to a professorship. Some contact was inevitable. And then Rowena Chote fell ostentatiously asleep at my inaugural. Comical, really, though I probably didn't think so at the time. I believe Lawford felt he had to compensate – show some extra friendliness.'

'I expect all of us have had snoozers in our lectures now and then,' Elvira said. 'I find the zonk-out rate for Cicero highest.'

'None of it has any bearing on our present task,' Mart said.

EIGHT

1987

On the way back from their sightseeing visit to Charter Mill, Lawford Chote said, 'That bastard.'

'Which?'

'Tane.'

'What's annoyed you, Principal?'

'Annoyed? That sounds like a carer to some half-witted antique wreck.'

'Angered, then,' Moss replied.

'Enraged,' Chote said.

'What's enraged you, Dr Chote?'

'Damn photography.'

'Photography? Which?'

'He had a photographer out at Charter recording the car. Didn't you see him?'

No, Moss hadn't seen him, if the photographer existed. In any case, if Mart *had* seen him he probably wouldn't have mentioned it. He didn't want to feed any of Lawford's obsessions. 'How could he know we'd be passing Charter to do our survey of the buildings and so on?'

'People at Sedge would have seen us leaving. Some traitor gets on his mobile to Tane.'

'People might have observed us leaving, but they wouldn't know where to, would they, Dr Chote?'

'Why else would he get a photographer in place with a damn sneaky camera? Someone at Sedge saw the departure and made a guess as to destination. It's a fairly obvious guess, isn't it?'

'Well, I don't know,' Moss replied.

'But *I* know. Oh, yes – he can't fool me.'

Moss sought some sanity. Had Chote tipped over? 'What would be the point in photographing us, anyway, Principal?'

'Don't ask me to read his damn twisted mind. He gets a picture of you and you're with me. That might suggest to his poisonous brain some sort of complicity.'

'But which sort?' Moss asked.

'Oh, yes, he'd be alert in his scheming head to signs of that category – or to what he could imagine were signs of that category. He's creating some kind of dossier.'

'But which kind?'

'Quite,' Chote replied.

NINE

1987

In the projection room at Charter Mill, Gloria Sondial, head of Organized Crime And Its Defeat, said, 'Principal, as part of our final year course we get students to carry out a covert surveillance exercise – one of the fundamental skills they'll need in a career with the police or security services.'

'Certainly,' Victor Tane replied.

'I've asked you kindly to spare some moments this morning, Principal, to look at a film one of our undergraduates took yesterday while carrying out that kind of work.'

'Delighted to, as it were, take part,' Tane said.

Gloria switched off the lights. 'First sequence, please, Alec. This is what we call "a situationer", Dr Tane,' Gloria said. 'It gives us a location, is a kind of context. In a surveillance operation, background can often tell plenty.'

'Right,' Tane said.

The technician started the film. A string of cars moved at speed limit pace across the screen, and then the camera swung away and showed some buildings. 'Oh, we're at Charter Mill, are we? There's the porter's lodge,' Tane said.

'Yes, we give the student a very familiar setting first and then, if he/she deals OK with that we'll put her/him in other, perhaps more complex, surroundings for subsequent tests. We know there are some good, semi-hidden spots to operate from here. Our people have to remain unobserved by the targets. The photos of the vehicles will show us whether the driver or passengers, if there are any, have spotted the camera and are gazing at it. If they do, the student is referred and must have another go at a later date before trying the more difficult stages. This exercise required the student to get a photographic record of six vehicles sequentially. Obviously, in a reality situation the camera would be aimed at one known vehicle only. That's not so in our present version. We go for a random six.'

Tane watched the screen as, first, a silver Ka with a woman driver passed, then a black Mercedes estate, an elderly male driving and a woman in the passenger seat, also elderly. A white Mazda 6 saloon, no passengers, a male driver, followed. None of the drivers or passengers seemed to notice the camera. After a pause a dark red Volvo, two men in the front seats, travelling very slowly appeared on the screen.

'Hold it there, Alec, would you please?' Gloria said, and the film froze.

'Ah, yes, I see,' Tane said.

'I wasn't sure I recognized either of them at first,' Gloria said, 'but I thought I might have seen media pictures of the driver. I know now it was when the TV news showed the Sedge principal with one of their ex-undergrads, later a decorated Falkland war hero, who came back to give a talk to students.'

'Yes, that's Lawford Chote,' Tane said.

'What struck me most about this view of the Volvo and its occupants wasn't so much the half-memory in my mind of one of them, but the way they both seemed to be examining the Charter Mill buildings and grounds – Chote less so than the passenger, of course, since Chote had the wheel, but I got the feeling that he was talking to the passenger, telling him where to look – as though they were on a sort of reconnaissance, sizing up the campus. The passenger is younger than Chote and it seemed to me that the Sedge principal might be introducing a subordinate to the kind of asset Charter Mill is, and accompanying this with some sort of commentary. They move slowly so as to take in as much detail as possible.'

'Yes,' Tane said. He leaned forward in his seat, studying the two faces in the Volvo.

The lights came on. Gloria was holding a clipboard. 'I asked two of our students to discover who the passenger is,' she said. 'This kind of tracking is another skill they'll most probably need in their careers – contributing to dossiers. They've come up with quite a full portrait.' She began to read from notes on the clipboard. 'He is Martin Calhoun Moss, born 1952 in Preston, married 1975 to Grace Shell, divorced 1980, no children. Graduated Cambridge 1973 (First, English Literature). Schoolmaster 1973-9, lecturer at Sedge 1979, prof 1987 – modern Eng and US lit. Address 4A Maliphant Close. Lives alone. Doesn't appear to be in any sexual relationship since divorce seven years ago. Drives a Vauxhall Astra, navy blue, 1981 model. Banks at Lloyd's. Is regarded by other staff at Sedge as a good and reliable colleague; not part of the clique known at Sedge as Chote's Chipper Chums, a kind of elite kitchen cabinet of unswerving henchmen and women, some of whom have been placed in newly created, executive posts by Chote to increase his clout.

This does not seem applicable to Moss. His promotion to a chair is the outcome of much published research on Wilde, Lawrence and Auden.'

'Yes, I've read some of his stuff. Bordering on the intelligible.'

Gloria said, 'It's speculation, not fact, Principal, but I'd guess that this Volvo trip is a preliminary to inviting Moss into that elite Chumdom.'

'I wondered about it,' Tane said. 'But what do you make of this trip, this "reconnaissance", apart from that?'

'I thought it looked like window shopping,' Gloria replied.

'How I saw it, too,' Tane replied.

Gloria gave him a couple of stills from the surveillance film and, back in his office, he gummed these into a log book he kept of his years as Principal of Charter Mill. He added a short caption for the pictures: names, location, source and date only. He felt that future developments could make any commentary he might have added look very off-beam and foolish. Of course, he had views about the Volvo and its crew – had agreed with Gloria's verdict – but backed off from writing anything down. It would be too committing. Careful, perhaps cagey, that was Tane. Occasionally, his caution bored even himself, but he was stuck with it, and knew this. Tall and unrobust-looking, he walked in a very tentative, doubting style, as if afraid there would be no floor for his next step.

Mart wondered whether Tane had been horrified as a kid by that scene in Robert Louis Stevenson's 'boy' novel, *Kidnapped,* where David Balfour, the hero, is climbing a staircase in absolute darkness and suddenly finds there is no further stair, only emptiness, into which he might have plunged. Perhaps that terror still affected Tane.

His receding, mousy coloured hair was brushed back hard over his ears. For someone who seemed so frail he had a surprisingly craggy face, though, with a wide-nostrilled Roman nose. Mart had heard that Tane spent plenty of mental energy trying to make sure his parents' quirks and foibles didn't in any fashion affect his present outlook on life.

TEN

2014

At the next statues meeting, Gordon Upp (Linguistics) said, 'I hope I'm not running ahead into quite complex, tricky matters before we've properly dealt with all the basics, but I wonder whether we should give some thought to what we might term the psychology – or, rather, *psychologies,* plural – of our two subjects, Chote, Tane – Tane, Chote – as they should be depicted in the statues. By psychologies I mean their mental make-up, their personalities, their spirits, their individual selfhoods.'

Upp would be under thirty years old, probably the youngest member of the committee. His moods swung about between extreme politeness and over-the-top pugnacity. He had a wide, heavy-jawed face. His gingerish eyebrows were much too sparse for this big area, like slivers of garden vegetation in a valiant but hopeless battle against some pesticide. His head hair, of the same colour, seemed comparatively healthy and worn long. He said, 'Lucy's very timely reference to the Aneurin Bevan statue over there in Wales goes some way towards what I'm getting at – *trying* to get at – Bevan's bodily stance as a kind of adjunct to his speechifying. But that is only what the Eng Lit people would term a *persona,* rather than his true unique *personality:* a pose, an assumed, theatrical-like, thesp-like, role, in harmony with one specific act – the speech – in one specific place – a political public meeting. Moments after doing his platform bit, he'd become someone else, not a spiel performer, but a bloke among other blokes and blokesses. I feel sure that each of us would wish the principals' statues to tell us something more profound, more fundamental, more, as it were, inborn than, for instance, Bevan's temporary, *ad hoc,* for-the-occasion, fighting posture. Somehow – and I certainly don't underestimate the difficulty of conveying this in a lump of stone or brass – but somehow the sculptor has to tell us of the differing, discrete qualities of these two men, not evaluations of them – this man good, or goodish, this one bad or baddish – but simply their abiding, congenital essences, their very fibre.

'I say "simply", but it is not at all a simple process. It is a massive challenge, or a pair of massive challenges in this instance. Although we are very wisely concerned to ensure equality between the statues – Tane, Chote – Chote, Tane – and although, also, each statue must tell the world of certain common qualities possessed by the two principals, crucial for men in their kind of leadership jobs – I mean, positivism, creative energy, devotion to learning – I feel it would be a mistake to make their facial expressions identical – both benignly smiling, for instance. A double helping of benign smiles if the statues are close to each other might be read by spectators as the result of a shared spliff or a heavy two-man session on the Jack Daniels. We need, rather, a comprehensive search into their very natures, and a due reflection of such in the statues. The character of Sedge itself should, to an extent, be blazoned in these statues.'

Lucy Lane (History) said, 'I promised last time to do a little browsing in the archives and I think I might have come across something with a bearing on what Gordon has just been talking about in his acute fashion. It is an item which rather directly involves Martin, our chair, too, and he will possibly be able to comment on it in a purely informative, unbiased fashion, without compromising his present office.'

'Oh?' Moss said.

'I'm sure it will activate memories although we are going to move back more than a quarter of a century.'

'Oh?' Moss said.

Lucy bent down and took what seemed to Moss like a large cardboard covered scrapbook from her briefcase. 'Victor Tane kept a kind of log of events in Charter Mill in 1987 and before and after, in what became the new Sedge,' Lucy said. She opened the book at around halfway. 'I think the fact that he did this tells us something about him. The log starts only from 1986, although Tane was in post at Charter several years prior to this. I could find no earlier log. I think his decision to begin the record when he did shows he realized something extremely major was happening, or was about to happen, and that a personal account of it day-to-day could be very to the point. He is perceptive. He is methodical. He is forward-looking. He is intelligently alert and, perhaps, self-protective.

'I'll pass the book around in a moment but I can tell you that it shows Principal Lawford Chote and our Professor Martin Moss in a red Volvo saloon on a piece of road which I thought I recognized. I went out to confirm it as being close to what was then Charter Mill, now one of the Sedge campuses. Chote is driving, Mart has the passenger seat. Although Chote is at the wheel his eyes are off the road ahead at the moment of the photograph. He is gazing at the Charter buildings in what seems to me an almost imperial style, noble and dauntless in its way, but, of course, hindsightedly poignant, ludicrous.'

Ollam said, 'If you're driving a Volvo the only hindsight available is through the rear-view mirror.'

'Imperial in which sense, Lucy?' Angela Drape asked.

'In the sense of colonising, in the sense of taking, of taking over.'

'"*Veni vidi vici*"?' Elvira said.

'"I came, I saw, I mean to conquer", and today I'll give Marty a briefing on it. "*Veni vidi vici*", Moss.' Lucy replied, laboriously deadpan. 'Chote's lips are apart and I think he might have been talking to Martin. No froth visible, but the tone of the messaging looks intense. This is something he should be able to clarify for the meeting soon.'

'What you seem to be telling us, Lucy, is that any statue of Lawford Chote must capture what you term the nobility and dauntlessness, while also suggesting that this seeming nobility, this seeming dauntlessness, are both, in fact, pathetically inappropriate and deeply frail when retrospectively viewed,' Theo Bastrolle (Business Studies) said. He'd be used to seeking a balance. 'I've been doing some archive research myself and have a similar impression,' Theo said.

'That complex mixture will be difficult to get in stone,' Upp said.

'Yes, how exactly does sculpting work?' Angela Drape asked. 'My training is in the actualities, the practicalities. Before he/she starts a bout of shaping does she/he say to himself/herself

over breakfast, I'll do some work on the nobility and dauntlessness aspects of the subject this morning? She/he sets off for
the studio, gets into dungarees and begins. If we were present
would we note that he/she was holding the chisel at a recom-
mended special angle for nobility and dauntlessness and
hammering it with a likewise particularly stipulated force for
nobility and dauntlessness – perhaps greater than usual, perhaps
less – so that after a couple of hours, or days, or even weeks,
carving like this she/he has knocked one area into a palpable
noble and/or dauntless area, ready to be slotted eventually into
the completed statue? Would he/she require a particular type of
stone, capable of being banged and chivvied into a nobility and
dauntlessness identity? And, even if the stone were absolutely
OK for the task, would the noble and dauntless sector have
to lie alongside another area or other areas, whose purpose is to
show that the incorporated chunks of sculpted nobility and
dauntlessness are of only limited account although she/he has
spent at least hours and possibly much longer battering and
chipping then into that wedge of stone?'

'Was Chote talking to you about take-over potential then,
Mart?' Bill Davey replied.

'I think of the devil showing Christ all the glories of the
world and declaring that the whole caboodle was there for
the taking if only Christ would bow down to him,' Elvira said.
'Gospel of St Matthew.'

'It's a long time ago,' Moss answered.

'Which, the forty days in the wilderness or the cherry-picking
trip to what was then Charter?' Jed said.

'In the pic, Martin, you look slightly bemused, guarded,
sceptical,' Lucy said.

'Well, if there's ever a statue of me it will have to show that
three-layered mélange of attitudes,' Moss said.

'Accompanying the pic is a note by Victor Tane,' Lucy said.
'It's economical to the point of terseness, as though he felt there
was no call to explain the photograph, other than to record
rock-bottom details – names, origin, date, time – because the
faces and the background location would tell everyone that this
was some sort of prospecting jaunt. "Care for a little trek Charter
Millwards in the Volvo, Mart?"'

'I wonder if the word *lebensraum* was mentioned at any stage,' Nelmes said.

'If Tane detected in Chote such an aggressive impulse we might have expected signs of resentment, anger, fear in the handwriting. But no,' Lucy said. 'The captions are very neatly done, label-like, no emotional swirls in the lettering, no screaming triple exclamation marks, no furious dashes or mid-sentence capitalisations. If he felt any menace he does not show it. Is this an indicator of Tane's confidence that, although Chote might turn up to remind himself of the plus elements in Charter, and to show a younger colleague the treats on offer, nothing would ever come of it? Or not that nothing would ever come of it, but that something *would* come of it, but this "something", the utter opposite of Lawford Chote's plan.'

Bill Davey said, 'Tane's statue, then, should radiate his calmness, self belief and contempt for Chote's dream, and Mart's dream, too, if he had become absorbed into Lawford's inner clique.'

'Had you been, Martin?' Jed asked.

'There was no need to take me out to have a stare at Charter. I'd often driven past it,' Moss replied.

'Yes, yes, but this time he probably wanted you to look at it as a possible target, as a potential prize,' Elvira said.

'Well, I can't say what he wanted,' Moss replied. 'You'd have to ask him.'

'It seems to me that ambiguity will be a required facet of the Tane statue,' Angela said. 'Can stone or brass do ambiguity?'

'Provenance?' Jed asked.

'Of what?' Lucy replied.

'The photograph. Why was it taken?' Jed said.

'They had a crime and detection department at Charter Mill,' Lucy replied. 'It might just be an exercise and the Chote inclusion simply a fluke.'

'So Tane is loved by Lady Luck,' Nelmes said. 'No wonder he won. Can statues be made to look lucky?'

'What's remarkable about this picture and the log,' Bastrolle (Business Studies) said, 'is that Tane left it for the archive. As you've described it, Lucy, this was a private journal kept by him for his own purposes. I would have expected Tane to take it with him on retirement, instead of which he makes it very accessible to posterity.'

'That's us,' Nelmes said.

'Of course, by the time of his retirement, he was Principal of the enhanced, enlarged Sedge,' Angela said. 'There's a subtle, crowing over Chote in Tane's making the pic, and, presumably, other material, open to inspection at the archive. The seeming neutrality and restraint are a front only, aren't they? He's really saying to anyone using the archive, to Lucy and via Lucy to the rest of us, "Get a look at this barmy, would-be invasive, Volvo-borne braggart, will you please?"'

'He's branding Chote a cunt, would you say, Ange?' Elvira (Classics) said.

'There'll be a need to get irony into the Tane statue, as well as all his other components,' Davey said.

ELEVEN

1987

'What we have to ask, Martin, isn't it, is who had availability at the specific time this morning?' Chote said.

In his head, Moss tried to analyse the principal's diktat. Mart reckoned he could have led a two-hour seminar deconstructing it. Which 'we' had to do the asking? Ask whom? Why the compulsion of '*have* to ask'? Why the awkward 'is' tangle in 'isn't it, is'? Which 'specific time'? Which 'availability'?

Chote had spoken in a very measured, matter-of-fact, calm, untroubled tone. Probably this meant the principal didn't feel at all calm and was severely troubled, Moss thought. Lawford had put in some excellent work on imitating normality. However, normality was not normal for him: normally he was abnormal. He seemed to sense that what he intended saying next might suggest unease or even paranoia, and he would guard against this. Did he suspect he must have sounded momentarily panicked and crazed about the photographer as they drove back from Charter earlier today and wanted to correct that? After lunch Chote's PA had phoned Mart in his departmental office and asked him to look in at the principal's suite as soon as he could.

Moss searched for enlightenment. '"Availability" in which regard, Principal?' he asked.

'Oh, yes, availability,' Chote replied. 'The very word! You've hit it exactly, Martin! The crux, surely.'

'Available to do what, though? "Availability" suggests there is some task or commitment which the available person, she or he, is available *for*.' He gave that some really dogged, plonking force. 'Availability' was getting the interrogation treatment.

'I'd like to take this matter very step-by-step and very logically, Mart,' Chote replied.

Which sodding matter? But Moss said, 'It's what people would expect of you, I'm certain.' And, yes, there might be some who would.

'This is a university,' Chote said.

Although the principal gave this a slight rise in intonation at the end, Moss took the words to be as a statement, not a question. 'Very true,' he replied. And it plainly was. Eu-fucking-reka!

'That might seem a barmily obvious comment but here's the point, Mart: proper, rational procedures are to be expected in such a setting. Are, in fact, *de rigueur*.'

'Definitely.'

'Thus, applying such rational procedures, I can state that if there were no availability there could be no action arising out of the availability,' Chote explained. 'There cannot be both availability and absence, one word cancelling out the other; and making the idea of possible shoulder-to-shoulderness absurd.'

'Agreed.'

'I've referred to step-by-step progress, and this recognition of the vital importance of availability is the first of these steps. Availability is a pre-requisite.'

'Understood,' Moss said.

'But you'll reproach me and say this is mere theorising and wind-baggery. Where is the example of this availability? A fair point, Martin. I admire your vigilance and clarity of thought.'

'Some disputation moves from the particular to the

general, some from the general to the particular,' Moss said. 'Each is valid. I think you are applying the second of these, Principal.'

'Absolutely, Mart. What this comes down to, finally, is of course, who? This is a wonderfully brief summation. Who?'

'Who in which particular?'

'Who had this availability that we've so far been discussing only as an abstract notion. The "who?" which we now ask, sharpens the topic, makes it specific. "Who", we inquire, "had this availability at the precise moment, moments." I don't say the answer to the "who?" is simple. We have to try to decide who among several possible whos. Here, then, comes the seminal question: who was available to see us move off in the Volvo this morning and give a call to that aspiring, window-dresser, Tane, informing him we were on our way, so he could get his damn filthy spy camera into place, ready to infringe on us?'

'Ah,' Moss replied, 'I get it, now: by "available" or "availability", you mean someone happened to be in a position to see us leaving in the Volvo.'

Chote's lips went into snarl mode, curling back over his teeth and showing entirely healthy, richly red, unbulbous gums. '*You* can say "happened" to be present and therefore available, Mart. That's not how I see it.' Lawford's voice was still mild and controlled, but Moss could detect a slight tremor there, perhaps from anger, perhaps from a fixation, perhaps from self-pity.

'We spoke about this in the car,' Moss said. 'No matter who saw us go, he/she wouldn't know to where. This is not like a bus with its destination shown in a frame up front. There'd be no apparent cause to phone Tane. What was there to say? "Principal Chote and Professor Moss have hit the road together in the same car." Well, hold the front page!'

'Let's put it like this, Martin. There was a ruthless plot to film us casing Charter Mill. Right?'

'Principal, this has not been totally established – not whether there was a plot at all, and, if so, a ruthless plot.'

'The creepy photographer is established, isn't he? You say you didn't see him. I did.'

'I accept that,' Mart replied. 'What isn't established is why he was there.'

'He's a photographer. He's there to take photographs.'

'But we cannot be sure why, Principal.' They had courses involving camera work over at Charter. A student might have been told to take some pics of traffic, as an exercise. By coincidence, the Volvo and its driver and passenger were possibly included in that traffic. From this, perhaps, flowed Chote's fierce suspicions.

'Tane told him to be there,' Lawford said, 'and to get shots of me, of us. Tane having been given the word that we're *en route* to do the casing. That's what Tane would call it. *We* might regard it simply as an innocent visit to look at Charter *in,* so to speak, *situ.* He'd say to the photographer – probably a student on one of their Dumbo courses, "Get into position near the entrance to the campus and, if you want to be given a degree here, don't come back without a picture of them – of them both, mind – both gawping at Charter and licking their sickeningly greedy lips."'

'Several imponderables here, if I may say, Principal,' Moss replied.

'Bugger imponderables.' Chote gazed about his office suite, as if seeking a spot uncorrupted by Mart's niggles and quibbles. It was a large room, with dark green wall-to-wall carpeting. The wallpaper also was mainly dark green, a kind of jungle theme: dense vegetation, stalks, fronds, branches, shrubs, possibly William Morris influenced. Chote sat at a long desk, one end of it containing his computer. Moss had a dark green leather armchair, near him. He felt it was like being in a bower, except for Chote who, to Mart, didn't seem a bower sort of person, even though he'd probably ordered the colour scheme.

'Yes, a plot,' Lawford said. 'And it worked, didn't it? How? Because there was a message from someone here saying that I and Profesor Martin Moss had gone journeying together in the principal's red Volvo. The recipient of that tip-off makes a guess, or a calculation, and decides the pair could be coming to Charter. It would be natural for someone like Tane to suspect this. He's jumpy. He's fearful. Rightly, he feels menaced by circumstances. Nerves savage him. He wants a record of the visit and as extra might get an identifying picture of a possibly new Lawford Chote associate – you, Mart. Tane orders the photo-surveillance and, we must suppose, achieves what he wanted. I would say – and I believe, Mart, that you will come to think the same – I would say that this completeness, this culmination, is the fruit of not just someone who "happened" by sweet fluke to be where she/he could observe our departure, but a someone who was uniquely "available" for that scheme, that plot, through the power of his/her instincts and magical opportunism. Hence my wish, Mart, my resolve, to check on availability.'

Martin Moss saw no 'hence', if hence meant, as it generally did, a reasonable, sane, deduction from what had gone before. Did Chote's apparent trust in instinct and magical opportunism indicate that he had gone full-out unhinged?

'Now, I think you'll grasp why I'm so concerned about availability, Mart,' the principal said. He picked up three A4 sheets of paper from his desk. 'I've done some private research.' He leaned forward and handed the pages to Moss. 'I believe you'll find them thought-provoking,'

Martin studied the top one. It had what appeared to be initials at the head: **R.S.G.**

Beneath these letters was today's date and then a column of figures:

0920–0940
0940–1000
10.00–10.20
10.20–1040
10.40–1100

Against 0920-0940 a typed note said: 'Room 17A, scheduled meeting with Estates Management Representatives.' Alongside the next two sets of figures, 0940-1000 and 1000-1020 was typed: 'Ditto, continuing.' Then, against 10.20 to 1040 and 1040 to 1100 a note said: 'No scheduled entries.' Moss glanced at the other two pages. They were set out in similar format, though the notation alongside the figures was different, and the capital letters at the top also varied.

'Do you see what they are, Mart?' Chote said.

'Well, not exactly,' Moss said.

'Which one are you looking at?'

'R.S.G.'

'Royston Stanley Gormand,' Chote replied. 'Roy.'

'What about him?' Moss asked.

'That's as near to timetabling his movements this morning as we can get. He had the diaried meeting with some estates people in 17A, diaried meaning it was entered in the departmental Appointments section. Availability you see, Mart. We can work out Roy Gormand's availability to some degree at least from his timetable. Such availability could begin at 1020.'

'Roy Gorman's availability as a traitor? But I thought Roy was one of your special—'

'I'm not sure of exactly what time we set out, you and I,' Chote replied, 'so I've tried to cover the complete 0920-1100 hours. I think we might have left at about 1025 or 30. I don't know if you can make it more precise than that. If you look on page 2, you'll see that C.L.M. – Carl Ivor Medlicott – lectured in B7 on 'Climate Irregularities In The Tundra' from 10 until 11, so, palpably, has no availability in the sense that interests us here. He can be eliminated from our survey, Martin. Contrariwise, Flora Dane Dinah Ellison had a pre-planned meeting with one of her post-grad students from 1000 until 1020, the rest of the period unaccounted for and therefore a possible as to the said availability.'

'But she might simply have been working alone in her room, before and after,' Moss said.

'Absolutely. Non-availability is undoubtedly conceivable. I might get telephone records to see whether she made or received calls during those uncharted minutes. If she did, it could clear her by proving what you've suggested. I want to be entirely fair, yet meticulously thorough.'

Gormand, Medlicott, Ellison: these were three of Chote's praetorian guard, his main and constant support. Moss sat bemused for some seconds, bemused and slightly scared at witnessing whatever it was that had taken Chote over. He had a very pale, long, aquiline face and it stayed pale and orderly now, showed no evidence of mental riot or bitter fantasising. How could that be?

'You're surprised at these names, I see,' Lawford said, his voice kindly, sympathetic. 'But a leader's closest associates know his strengths and weaknesses best and might be more able than any others to use that knowledge to neutralize those strengths, exploit those weaknesses. Think of rulers killed by their bodyguards.'

Mart thought, instead, of the John le Carré espionage novels: the obsessive line on betrayal in the Secret Service, and the hunt for a traitor among seeming colleagues and friends. Lawford Chote appeared to be taking that obsessiveness one stage further: into mania. 'Availability to carry out some action is not the same as actually carrying it out, Principal,' Moss said.

'Of course it isn't,' Chote replied. 'It is a necessary preliminary to that action, though. I must watch these three. Perhaps you will help me in this, Mart? I don't need an immediate answer. But give it thought, will you, please? We are talking about the well-being of Sedge. We may have in our care its safety, its continuing life, indeed. You may keep the papers for study and reference. They might help you realize the seriousness of the threat confronting us. The lists of times look so routine and harmless, yet what might they hide, Mart? Yes, what indeed?'

TWELVE

1987

Of course, the injuries and general chaos that ended the banquet to mark Sedge's centenary should have been foreseen. And, to be fair to himself, Mart Moss *had* expected some turbulence there, some joshing and teasing. What happened went way beyond this, though. Surely, nobody would have predicted such violence. Although the setting could hardly have been more dignified, time-blessed and uplifting, this failed to inspire a due response from some of the guests. Moss suspected they had deliberately planned their vandalism in advance. This wasn't just a lark, spontaneous and childish, but well-organized destructiveness.

The banquet took place in the magnificent Plain Parlour of Standfast Fort. This nicely restored and preserved castle dated from Tudor times and stood in the city centre. It was famous throughout the county and beyond for hosting high-grade knees-ups in its Plain Parlour. Standfast had been prominent during the seventeenth-century Civil War, on the Royalist side. At one stage it was, in fact, overrun by some of Oliver Cromwell's troops and most histories of the period said Plain Parlour saw hand-to-hand fighting and even bloody deaths. No deaths now, but some scrappping.

The regrettable behaviour at the Sedge centenary do was not caused by people wanting to re-enact in a playful, modern-dress way those Civil War ructions, but arose out of very contemporary opposed views and lively hatreds. The hiring charge for Plain Parlour, a bar and staffing was already steep. Damage and breakages caused to salvers, tureens and general crockery, to the lighting system, to some mahogany panelling (this disputed), and to chairs used as weapons and/or missiles, pushed the bill higher still. In any case, could it be altogether sane to put on this lavish function now? Martin would concede that it would honour Sedge's one hundred years of existence and achievement, a very worthy aim; but also very expensive. Sedge would be stuck with the complete festive costs at a time when its finances were rumoured to be overstretched, perhaps terminally overstretched. Back at Sedge there might one day be fighting as rough as any ever witnessed in Plain Parlour, but it would be against bailiffs, not Roundheads.

It hadn't happened yet, though, and the jubilee proceeded. There had been several serious attempts to stop it altogether or, at least, to keep it modest and comparatively cheap. Lawford didn't do modesty and despised anything cut-price. But, after all, 100 was no great age for a university: England and Europe had colleges and universities that went back to the Middle Ages. Luther lectured at Wittenberg in the early 1500s. Moss knew about one of these doomed efforts to cancel or shrink the pageantry because he had been involved in it – unwillingly and more or less accidentally involved, but involved just the same.

He'd had a phone call on a Sunday morning at home in Maliphant Close from someone who said he was Ned

Lane-Hinkton of the U.F.C. (Universities Finance Centre). 'I'm coming down to Sedge tomorrow, Mart, and I wondered if we could meet up.'

Moss had been startled to get what he assumed was a business call on a Sunday; surprised, too, that he should get a call at all from the U.F.C. This wasn't his kind of terrain. He wouldn't have thought anyone at the U.F.C. could even have heard of him, a non-Oxbridge Humanities prof, let alone address him by his shortened first name and suggest they 'meet up'. Why 'up'? Wasn't it only Americans who met *up*? Brits met.

'To do with what?' Mart had said.

'May I ask you to book somewhere for lunch?' Lane-Hinkton replied. 'Not the famed Sedge dining room, nor anywhere on university ground. Somewhere reasonably discreet in the town.'

'Somewhere secret?'

'Discreet. If poss. Know anywhere like that?'

Moss gave him the name of a dockside pub where he and his wife used to eat now and then before the divorce. He couldn't remember ever seeing anyone he knew lunching there.

Lane-Hinkton turned out to be fat, jolly-looking, his voice confiding. The words arrived unrushed from one side of his mouth, varying right or left, depending not on the political flavour of what he was saying, but simply on where his listener, listeners, was, were. Moss thought Lane-Hinkton – ('Ned, or Neddy, please, Mart') – was abour twenty-seven or -eight, unmoustached, apparently untattooed, teeth his own and well looked after, very dark hair, pony-tailed and bound at the back with a plastic clasp of some sort. He was short, physically slow-moving, blue-black eyes, mouth open more often than not, as if he had trouble getting enough oxygen to his lungs, although his tongue looked radiantly hale. He wore shiny grey leather trousers, a pale red linen jacket, weighty brown, lace-up shoes, most probably advertised as 'water-repellent'. Under the jacket he had on a formal white shirt with ruffles across the chest, a stiff collar and bow tie, one wing of it purple, the other turquoise.

He was already at a table in The Lock Gate when Moss arrived and rose to welcome him. 'Mart,' he said, 'grand to see you.' Moss was to his left as he came into the dining room and

Ned's greeting was from that side of his mouth: the bow tie's purple side. 'Lovely place. They've got black-pudding hash on as Meal of the Day, one of my very favourites. Worth travelling from London for. One can get it in smart joints there, yes, but I always feel they're doing it to show they know how to go basic peasant once in a while. Here, though, it seems natural. Quite possibly the black pud is top range Irish, maybe Clonakilty. Unbeatable. *So* eatable.' He held out his hand and Moss shook it. Three other tables were occupied. 'I'd have recognized you anywhere, Mart,' Ned said.

'How?'

'The photo. Damn clear. A professional, I shouldn't wonder. You, gazing very hard at the surrounds, obviously on a kind of survey.'

'Which photo?' Moss replied. So Lawford had been right.

Ned sat down and Martin took the other chair. 'Volvo,' Lane-Hinkton said. 'A copy came our way the way these things will in their own fashion, won't they, Mart?'

'Will they? Which way will they come in their own fashion?'

'In one sense it's the photo that brings me here,' Lane-Hinkton said.

'Which?'

'What?'

'Sense,' Mart replied.

'I can't say it was the black-pudding hash because I didn't know it would be on until I got here.' He laughed mildly to offset the clunking plod of this logic.

'In what sense, then, Ned?'

He had the remains of his chuckle still softening the line of his lips. 'In confidence, Mart, I prefer Neddy. It has that nursery touch about it; a toddler's affectionate cognomen. People feel safe with me. They relax. I can surprise and floor the stupid sods by suddenly turning so fucking uncongenial and ruthless.'

'Right, Neddy,' Martin replied.

'Oh, I don't include you, Mart.'

'Include me in what?'

'As one of those stupid sods who can be fooled by a crude stratagem, viz, sticking a couple of extra letters on to Ned. You'd see through it.'

'Is this another stratagem?' Mart asked.

'Which?'

'To say I'd never be fooled by that cruder strategem,' Moss said.

'God, Mart, this conversation could go on and on, like the never-ending line of Banquo's ghosts in *Macbeth*. We must focus on our main topic. The ride out to Charter was a special quest, wasn't it? I've said a survey. Inventorying? We are inclined to regard it as one of those rites of passage – you'll know the Golding novel of that title, naturally – something that possibly changes a life in the most profound style.'

'Which we?'

'And for a special quest he took a special guest: your very self, Mart. This would seem to proclaim a relationship – not a relationship in the *relationship* usage of *Lady Chatterley's Lover* – about which more later – but a relationship of a work-related, professional, drift.' Lane-Hinkton shook his head. It was severe reproof of himself. 'Do forgive me, Mart, but I seem to be taking charge in a pushy, metropolitan way. Because *I* fancy the black-pudding hash so unambiguously, so vividly, so convinced that the onion-potato ratio of the hash will be perfect, I'm assuming you will fancy it, too. Arrogance! There's liver and bacon, also, which, had there not been the black-pudding hash, I would have gone for. And this might well be your choice. Or they have a vegetarian course, or skate, or lasagne. Don't let me bully you, Mart! I trend in that direction, I'm afraid. On my personnel dossier at U.F.C. there's probably a note: "Ned is inclined to bully re black-pudding hash." Wilt take some ale, or an Old Raj gin and bitters. I checked that they have max alc Old Raj.'

'There's a photo?' Mart replied.

'Well, as I said, Martin, it's the photo that prompted the visit. Geraldine – she and I are the "we" – Geraldine thought I should come and have a word. And, clearly, what Geraldine in her newly enhanced power role at U.F.C. says goes. A moot, a suggestion, is an edict. Also clearly, what she is looking for, what, indeed, the whole of U.F.C. is looking for, is a convenient way to reach this maverick sod, Chote. When I say convenient, what I mean is a mode of reaching him which doesn't touch off all his extreme and negative reactions leading to impasse. The time for impasses has passed, Mart, I think you'll agree. There should no longer be impassible impasses.'

'Reaching him?'

'Get through to him. Get his attention. Get him to hear the warnings and respond rationally to them, not detonate or spit and/or sulk.'

'Which warnings?'

'Geraldine envisages a sort of go-between service,' Ned replied. 'But don't take that as a slight, will you? This would be, will be, a crucial liaison role, with enormous implications. We need someone, and you seem wonderfully well suited, Mart. Cohabitation of the Volvo on that keynote saunter sends us this signal. Geraldine schemes a sort of devious, though legitimate, approach to Lawford. When Geraldine writes her memoirs they'll be titled *The Compleat Wangler.*'

Moss loved lunchtime drinking. Afternoons could be memorably or non-memorably improved by it. He'd come by bus and would get a taxi back. The English department had no teaching on Mondays. Traditionally it was regarded as a wind-down day after the weekend. But, by quick, intelligent adaptation, it could be used, too, as a weekend extension day, if, for example, a good lunch materialized. Ned must realize this about university Humanities departments or he wouldn't have suggested the feed.

He had the kind of teeth that would tell black-pudding hash who was boss. He and Mart both downed Old Raj and bitters to kick off with, then a bottle of Chilean white between them for the first course, kedgeree, and a claret magnum with Ned's black-pudding hash and Mart's liver and bacon. Mart took a half bottle of Sicilian Corvo with the cheeseboard and Ned had a bumper glass of Barsac for the sticky toffee pudding.

During the main, Ned said in very kindly though not sloshed tone, 'There's quite a bit of affection for Lawford at U.F.C., flagrant shit-or-bust arsehole though he might be, Martin. We sincerely wish to help him and Sedge. Swapsies? I'll give you a mouthful of my hash so you may marvel at the ingredients' balance, and I will take a token square of your liver-tinged bacon.'

For a moment Mart wanted to reject this idea, afraid that, when Ned said he would give Mart a hash mouthful, Lane-Hinkton meant his own mouthful. This to be delivered to Moss's mouth by lips contact and a controlled disgorging from Ned's right or left mouth area depending on how he felt it best to approach Mart as to tilt for the transfer – a move something like one motherly aircraft refuelling a small-fry plane in flight.

But Ned meant only a cutlery-based exchange of samples, a piece of black-pudding garnished with hash from him, a strip of liver-boosted bacon from Mart. He'd had the black-pudding hash here on one of his visits with Grace and had found the hash too dense, and still did, though he said, 'Excellent, yes. Oh, yes!' And Ned praised the augmented bacon. Moss thought Neddy might regard this mutual mouthful savouring as a kind of blood-brothers bonding ritual. People spoke of 'breaking bread' with someone as a sign of abiding inter-dependence and friendship. This would be 'breaking black-pudding hash' or 'liver-partnered bacon', but perhaps Lane-Hinkton saw their across-the-table, non-drip forkings as a similar symbolic pledge of shared purpose and comradeliness.

'It's your newness, you see, Mart. This is what Geraldine homed in on. That's one of her attributes – to home in on essentials. She doesn't care for lav language, but if she did she would probably have as her motto "cut the crap". As it is, she speaks of "getting to the inner".'

'Is that where I am?' Moss replied.

'We can't go to Roy Gormand or Flora Ellison or Medlicott, Chote's clique of cliques people, his devotees. They're cowed. We wouldn't be sure they'd do the job in the fashion it needs to be done.'

'Which job? Which fashion?'

'The warnings. Categorical.'

Lane-Hinkton had brought complexities with him, as well as dress style. Chote's clique of cliques, his devotees, were not relied on by Geraldine or Ned to 'reach' him, 'get through' to him, and they wanted Mart for that. But, alongside this, Chote's attitude to his clique of cliques, his devotees, was troubled because he suspected one of them – more than one? – had given the treacherous word that put the cameraman in place and, apparently, produced a Volvo pic. Mart felt tugged in two directions, one to be Ned and Geraldine's man and 'reach' Lawford; and, two, to be Lawford's man and hunt down the spy or spies, if they existed, which, on balance, he thought they didn't. Mart took a decidedly forceful swig of the claret – though from his glass, not the magnum bottle – a swig to clear his head, or to take him to an afternoon men's spot where he didn't have to worry whether his head were clear or not. Or even whether it was still there.

'This meal, for instance, Mart.'

'Always reliable.'

'Oh, true. But, no, not this one.'

'Which?'

'The Sedge Centenary feast,' Lane-Hinkton said.

'In Plain Parlour?'

'Geraldine thinks it must not go ahead. Or not go ahead on the proposed scale.'

'The thing about things . . . Sorry . . . The thing about events at Plain Parlour, Neddy, is that they have to be of a due grandeur and shape. The surroundings demand it. That kind of setting must be lived up to or the occasion's a contemptible flop. History requires it, surely. The Charles aspect. The Cromwell aspect.'

'This is why I referred to warnings, Martin. I'm not one to look down on history and neither is Geraldine, to my knowledge. The reverse in my own case. But, just as in hash, ratio is so important, and is acknowledged by you as admirable in the present dish, so there has to be a satis ratio between history and the present fucking dark situation menacing Sedge, owing to distortions in the ratio of Chote's splendid leadership flair on one hand, and respect for the dictates of income and cash generally – or their looming lack – on the other. Now, Mart, I don't want you to think I ordered the black-pudding hash merely to make a clever-clever allegorical point about potato-onion ratio and university governance. That would be a disgustingly calculating ploy. The black-pudding hash is brilliant in its own right, in its own Lock Gate right, as

appreciatively endorsed by you. But the comparison of the
hash and the Sedge Principalship came to me just now as a
sudden revelation and I felt duty-bound to mention it. Perhaps
I'm using imagery in the metaphysical poets' fashion, where,
at first sight the two sides of a metaphor seem utterly unlike,
rather than like each other – for instance, the human body as
a dungeon, in Andrew Marvell; or black-pudding hash and the
principal of a university, here – but on second thought
the resemblance is clear and striking.'

Ned got another piece of black-pudding on to prongs and
rubbed it gently around his plate to add another hash smear,
then offered it as before to Mart, a kind of refresher in the
ratio discussions. Moss thought he'd better take it, for frater-
nity's sake. He had a degree of difficulty in getting his mouth
to exactly where the tidbit was but eventually managed this
acceptance OK without disturbing any of the other customers
too much. He greatly liked The Lock Gate, even though Grace
didn't accompany him any longer, and he would hate to
be banned. This was the chief reason he'd repressed the impulse
to drink straight from the claret magnum just now. Mart reckoned there was something at least impolite and possibly crude
about drinking wine from a magnum in a public area. After
a while he responded with a bacon-liver montage remnant for
Lane-Hinkton. Ned didn't seem able to get a simile of any
sort from this part of the menu to put extra light on the Sedge
predicament, thank God.

'It's like giving the finger to U.F.C.,' Ned said.

'What is?'

'Plain Parlour. The outlay.'

'Geraldine knows about it?' Mart asked.

'Lawford has asked her to pencil in the date. Naturally,
she'll be invited. Obligatory. She is one of U.F.C.'s main
figures. The Plain Parlour carry-on will be using U.F.C. money,
won't it, Mart, unless Geraldine puts a stopper on funding?
This is within her power-range now – why I mentioned the
enhancing. But I don't think she'd wish to cut off the boodle
like that. Peremptory, Mart. That's how she'd regard such an
extreme move: peremptory, contrary to the wholesome ethos
of university education in G.B. Consider the likely media

treatment of such a disaster. "FAMED CENTURION UNI SKINT", and then a list of distinguished Sedge alumni with grieved and/or angry quotes about the impending death of a fine, beloved *alma mater.*

'And so she'd like you to talk to Chote and highlight the . . . the tensions. Geraldine considers that there is no sexual element in Chote's special attention to yourself. I hope that doesn't disappoint you, Mart. She's had some inquiries made and finds that Lawford greatly appreciated your reaction to Rowena Chote's trumpet-tone dossing during a lecture you gave on Lawrence and the Mellors-Connie shag experimentation. This is what made him interested in you.

'Perhaps Chote had been feeling that his closest gaggle of minions were, are, no longer coming up with sparkling ideas for Sedge's progress; perhaps, even back then at the lecture, he wondered about the loyalty of one of them, or more. Principal Chote is ready to turn elsewhere in his search for major support, and, suddenly, at a standard inaugural spiel about Connie Chatterley's widening romantic experience, sees what he imme- diately regards as a gifted possible aide, Mart Moss. Now, of course, Mart Moss is not entirely new to him. Mart Moss has moved up the grades over the years to a professorship, and Chote has been Principal there for some of those years. But the night of the lecture brought a revelation to Lawford about said Martin's qualities, Mart.

'Here is someone strong and confident enough to carry on his performance through a snores blitz by the principal's piss- artist wife; a glistening achievement in itself, but, capping this, he has the ability to reach in to the deep recesses of Rowena's kip, and freight her back to lively, fascinated consciousness by flagging up unconventional fuckings among the clucking game bird chicks. Chote possibly blamed himself for not recognising your talents, Mart. This is why, as a kind of reparation, a kind of self-correction, he takes you on the Volvo mission. He believes in you, Mart. Hence, you are someone of serious power and valuable influence. We inevit- ably recognize that this might be a temporary matter, only. But then, life is only a temporary matter, isn't it? Geraldine wouldn't want to be other than straightforward about this.

We've seen what's happened to Gormand and the others. They have their little day and that's it.

'Geraldine wants to avail herself of your favoured position while it is so. She is confident you can persuade Lawford into restraint, into acumen, into self-salvation. Geraldine said she would bet a cool 20p that at no stage during this drive was Chote's hand on your knee or higher, that this was not a wooing or grooming jaunt in the Volvo, but a testament to your harmonising with his professional and business attitude, a harmonising which we dearly want to avail ourselves of, Mart, in an attempt to divert Lawford Chote and the university you all worship from catastrophe.'

They took a couple of Kressmann Armagnacs with their coffees. Ned said, 'From the Condom area.'

'How do you mean? What is?'

'The Armagnac. Condom, West France. And then there's Rowena, of course.'

'Is there?'

'She might feel just as indebted to you as is Lawford on account of disrespectful, ostentatious sleeping while you gave your inaugural. Perhaps she still harbours guilt about that and is keen to make up for it.'

'I haven't ever noticed any sign of guilt.'

'Of course you haven't, Mart, because, as we understand it, she came out of the slumber into sheer perkiness and joy at your delicious exposition of wayward, all-round sex. That's the aspect of her you see. But there could be others. You have captured the esteem of both a wife and her hubby. This is a terrific accomplishment. And now, surely, as well as your direct route to Lawford you can call on Rowena to help in trying to talk him out of mad money-chucking at Standfast.'

'She's said something like that to me, asking for help. My impression of Rowena is she'll always back Lawford in whatever he proposes.'

'That would be her initial instinct, yes. But, Mart, you have her ear. At least her ear.'

THIRTEEN

2014

'I've been casting my mind back,' Lucy Lane said.

'Well, that's what historians are supposed to do,' Nelmes said with a kindly smile.

'Touch-*bloody*-é,' Lucy replied, also smiling. 'But not very far back – only very, very recent history. Ours. Plinths. The previous discussion of.'

'As I recall it, the plinth matter was left unresolved,' Moss said.

'So it was, Mr Chair,' Lucy said.

'Our discussion was about entitlement,' Gordon Upp said, 'turning on whether one or both rated a plinth. No, "rated" is probably the wrong term – certainly *is* the wrong term, since it suggests a ranking of plinths whereas plinths are really much of a muchness. In any case, the general feeling was that if Chote had a plinth Tane must have one, and of course, contrariwise.'

'Exactly,' Lucy Lane said. 'Now, what I'd like to ask is what was the prevailing, though unspoken, background presumption here?' She put some merriment into her voice, as if running a quiz for primary school children. Lucy left her nose contents undisturbed, probably intent on giving full attention to the poser she'd set; no matter what her nostrils had ready to be fished out, she could not allow this distraction now. Martin thought she might want to escape for a while the 'historian' label just fixed on her and get into the bustling, intriguing present.

'The presumption?' Bill Davey replied. 'It was that each principal deserved to be honoured via a statue.'

Lucy did a brief, minor handclap. 'Absolutely. But I'd like you to note two words there,' she replied. She paused. 'Which two words, you might ask?'

'Or maybe not,' Jed Laver said.

'Well, I won't toy with you, tease you,' Lucy replied. 'The two words are, of course, "each" and "a".'

'Naturally,' Laver said. 'They always bring with them a special glow. They really stand out, "each" and "a". Where would eloquence and oratory be without them? Hearing them we know we're in touch with a vocabulary.'

'OK, OK, take the piss if you must, Jed. What do the two imply, though?' Lucy said.

'Well, they look harmless enough, in the context,' Elvira Barton said. 'We're not going to get a lot of aggro from a word such as "a".'

'"In the context" is so right,' Lucy said. 'What *is* their context, Elvira? Forgive the doggedness, but I feel I must push on towards a worthwhile truth.'

'The context?' Elvira replied. 'Statues.'

'Spot on!' Lucy said.

'And their plinths,' Wayne Ollam said.

'I was taking their plinths for granted,' Elvira said.

'But can we?' Theo Bastrolle asked. 'Plinths are not a simple, subordinate, on-the-nod matter.'

'Plinths don't grow on trees,' Jed said. 'In fact, if anyone can cite a country where plinth trees grow I'll pay a grand to the charity of his or her choice.'

'Bill's observation was that "each principal deserved to be honoured via a statue",' Lucy said. 'The "each" and the "a" refer to single, solo entities, don't they – "each" principal, "a" statue. But if we put them together, as is done in Bill's typically perceptive remark, we have a plural, a duality, don't we? Because there are two principals and each must have a statue, it's clear that there must also be two statues – and, incidentally, two plinths. This is why I mentioned the context as being important. And now, here – a little late, I'll agree – is my point. It seems to me that in our conversations we have always assumed two separate statues and, accordingly, two separate plinths. I want to question this. In fact, we *must* question this.'

'You Cambridge graduates, so driven by rigour,' Wayne Ollam said. Yes, Lucy's light-hearted tone had been displaced now.

'What are you saying, Lucy – that there should be only one statue – singular, not plural?' Elvira asked. 'Surely we all agreed very early on in our meetings that fairness and, indeed, justice demanded there should be two.'

'We did, we indeed did,' Lucy said. She smiled again, plainly about to suggest something that would roughly shake at least some of their previous plinth thinking.

'Well?' Elvira said.

'We indubitably must have two statues,' Lucy said, 'but my mind lately has been relentlessly asking, do we need two plinths rather than one? Do we *have* to think binary? Are two compulsory?'

'But that has also been covered in our discussions on fairness and equality,' Jed Laver said.

'It has, it has,' Lucy replied. 'However, our premise then was that there would be two statues at different locations. In this case, to deprive one principal of a plinth would appear biased, partial, uncivil. There had to be a parity of plinths.'

'Am I reading you right, Lucy?' Angela Drape asked with something of a gasp.

'Are you?' Lucy replied impishly.

'You're putting in front of us the notion that there should be *one* plinth only and both statues should be on it,' Bill Davey said.

'You've got it, Bill,' Lucy said.

'Buddy, can we share a plinth?' Laver said.

'That would require them to be very close to each other, perhaps even touching,' Bill said.

'Our intended theme is unity, isn't it?' Lucy said.

'That's its public face, yes,' Bill said.

'Public faces are what we are concerned with, Bill, the public faces of statues – faces and the other parts of the imitation bodies. We want to preach a grand message of accomplishment through what? Through cooperation,' Lucy said. 'Is there a better way of doing this than to have the two men jointly responsible for this unity and accomplishment standing proudly together, blazoning sculpturewise that superb harmony by their comradely togetherness on a shared plinth?'

'Like Abbott and Costello,' Angela said.

'Who?' Lucy said.

'In a way that's quite a promising comparison,' Elvira said.

'These were two comedy stars in the 1940s and 50s. Their films come on the movie channel now and then. The underlying motif is that neither is complete without the other. They are complementary facets of one personality, facets which are not always in accord, but which are complementary all the same.'

'Sort of Abello,' Laver said.

'Similarly, George Burns and Walter Matthau in *The Sunshine Boys*.' Elvira replied. 'Another vaudeville comedy duo who score off each other in their act, and even in real life, but there is the same sort of implied powerful bond. They need each other.'

'Clown and straight man?' Laver asked.

'Perhaps we shouldn't go too closely into that at this juncture,' Elvira said.

'Which juncture *is* it?' Bill said.

'Speculative,' Elvira replied.

Theo Bastrolle said, 'OK, well let's speculate a bit further. Under Lucy's plan—'

'Well, only an idea for now,' Lucy said.

'Under Lucy's idea the two of them cohabit a plinth. How do they inter-act, given this proximity?' Theo asked.

'They're stone or brass,' Ollam said. 'Limiting for interaction.'

'But they are stone or brass copying life,' Lucy said. 'They are like all art – in this case sculpture – yes, all art seeks to, as it were, capture in one glimpse of the subject, one view of a scene, one record of a facial expression, one attitude of a body, a whole statement about the context – there's that word again – a statement about the context, the setting, that has provided this scene, that facial expression, the bodily attitude. The statues are what Eliot might term "objective correlatives".'

'Ouch!' Laver remarked, 'take me back to "each" and "a".'

'Would they be looking at each other on the plinth in sort of mutual respect, even affection, for each other?' Gordon Upp said. 'Like that song, "Me and my Shadow"?'

'It would certainly not answer the problem if they were shown staring at each other with contempt and/or hatred,' Angela said. 'Too much truth can become . . . well, too much.'

'Or perhaps not looking at each other as plinth passengers, but gazing out in different directions, their bodies, especially feet, inevitably plinth-close but angled away from each other, as if to signal the marvellously holistic nature of universities,' Lucy said, 'their . . . well . . . universality of outlook and aim. Obviously, I think of that line in, I think, a Robert Bridges poem, addressing a handsome, wind-driven vessel: "Whither away, fair rover, and what thy quest?",' Lucy said. 'Each principal having been an intellectual "rover" in his fashion, voyaging forward on his own individual quest, mainsails hoisted, that quest in both cases being the enhanced reputation, glory, continuance of Sedge.'

'But, of course,' Nelmes said, 'neither of them will be looking towards a horizon, if we go for this kind of tableau. They are not aboard that great questing ship with a vast empty expanse ahead of them, just perfect for whithering away into with a full spread of canvas. This is a built-up area. Depending on the nature of their stance they will be as if taking a long glance at certain specific urban features. And the contemporary viewers of the statues should, I imagine, be able to catch something of each principal's character by noting what he is deemed to be gazing at, what interests him. The point with statues, of course, is that once their eyes are fixed on something they have to stay fixed. A statue can't look back over his or her shoulder if worried about being stalked, unless, that is, the statue from the start is of someone looking back over her/his shoulder, not a common statue style, however. Rodin's *Le Penseur* might have thoughts ranging in all kinds of directions, as is the nature of thoughts, but the statue has him facing strictly ahead and a bit downwards.

'So, for instance, perhaps the Lawford Chote would have his eyes settled on the new, executive-style housing estate a little way out of the city centre at Cottle Realm. This might indicate that Chote approved of superior, modern domestic architecture, and admired the self-bettering push that enabled people to shell out for such pricey properties. Or, of course, it could be Tane who felt like that about the estate. The other statue, whichever it might be, could seem very fascinated by the mixed sex Brade Academy playing fields nearby, exciting tourneys of netball, lacrosse and so on. That could be an entirely innocent, whole-some, matter but might tell us something about the leanings of one of them, Chote or Tane or Tane or Chote.'

Angela twitched a bit, then boomed, 'If they were plinth-linked as in Lucy's scheme, we have to ask about location.'

'Location?' Lucy replied.

Angela said, 'Sedge, as it exists now, is one university but with two campuses – what was Charter Mill and what was Sedge. Now, though, Charter Mill as a title is extinct, though the Charter Mill buildings and so on are very much with us; perhaps in one sense more with us than is the original separate Sedge, since the merger became possible only because Charter remained brilliantly solvent, even in its controlled, unflamboyant way, thriving. To continue the maritime imagery, Charter under Tane was the lifeboat that rescued Sedge in its previous, drifting, wrecked form, Captain Chote still on the bridge, the engine room telegraph set at Full Ahead, but with no engines. Where, then, should any double-item tribute stand – in front of the city centre Sedge complex, on view to many; or at the outlying former Charter unit with its *prima facie* case to be the core constituent of our present day Sedge?'

Lucy said, 'Naturally, I've already considered this difficulty. My thinking is that conjunctive statues on their single plinth might easily be transported between each campus and estab-lished at one or the other for, say, a sixth month or annual spell. There could be an impressive ceremony at the arrival of the statues for their stint at this or that site, like the changing of the guard at Buck House.'

'Wouldn't this here-today, gone-tomorrow policy suggest nervousness, even confusion, about the stability of the new Sedge?' Elvira asked. 'How would the statues be dressed? This is a matter we haven't dealt with yet. But if Chote and Tane or, alternatively, Tane and Chote, are going to be in doctoral robes with mortar boards and tassels, carted back and forth on the back of a lorry across the city at switchover dates, they'll look like aristos getting tumbrilled off to Madame Guillotine.'

'There would have to be a recognized resting place for the plinth at each campus, a concrete platform, and how depress-ingly voided and abandoned that would seem at whichever of the campuses were without the statues for the ordained period,' Angela said.

Lucy said, 'I thought there could be an inscription cut into the concrete: "We shall return" – a slight adaptation of General Douglas MacArthur's "I shall return" when he escaped from the Japanese in the Philippines during the Second World War. This would be a positive factor, not the reverse. That "we" captures the wonderful conjoint purpose. It is a promissory note sure to provoke anticipation of their assured reappearance in this reserved, designated spot.'

FOURTEEN

1987

'I know you'll forgive this . . . this . . . well, I think it must be termed subterfuge, or intrusion, at least, Martin. I can't even say it's well-meant. No, impossible to say that. The thing is, we don't feel 100 per cent private, secure, back there in the buildings, as it were. You've probably noticed that a dire sort of atmosphere has, regrettably, begun to prevail, an atmosphere hard to define, but obviously to do with acute anxieties, anxieties bordering on fear, and, in addition, something sickly, something toxic and disabling. We're certain we'd feel inhibited there, given the nature of what we want to discuss with you.

'And so we thought we'd take the chance – see if we could catch you at home. This is presumptuous, perhaps – presumptuous in the sense that it might be deeply inconvenient for you. If it is, Martin, please say so at once. We'll vamoose. We'll not be offended. We quite recognize that it's outstanding good luck to find you here, answering the doorbell to an unannounced call. For us to then go further and demand a slice of your time is beyond presumptuous. It's super-presumptuous.' She paused and for a second put her hand over her mouth, as if to silence herself. 'But, I say, what a spiel this is on your doorstep, Mart! I've gone blabby.'

And, yes, she bloody had. 'Come in, do come in,' Moss replied with gorgeous affability.

'May we, really? We're not a nuisance? I hope you won't think we're ganging up on you – the two of us in a combined, double-pronged approach.'

'Please,' Martin said. He led them into the sitting room. He didn't see how this visit could be other than extensively bad for him. Their need for 100 per cent privacy and security unsettled him. The lavish, galumphing politeness put him on guard. He wished he hadn't made them lucky by opening the door. Yes, he *did* suspect this visit to be a double-pronged approach, a double-pronged attack, the old one-two.

'As you'll no doubt have gathered, I elected myself spokesperson for the early moments at any rate. Well, you might say, it seemed a lot more than moments – yes, elected myself as icebreaker spokesperson,' Flora Ellison said.

'I knew Flora would make a better fist of it than I possibly could,' Roy Gormand said, 'her flair for summing up a situation in a few meaningful words.'

'Comparatively few,' Flora said.

'Summing up and clarifying,' Gormand said. 'No matter how complex that situation might be Flora will provide a simplified version, missing none of the essentials.'

'Such a lovely room – the sense of space and yet also of comfort,' Flora said, doing a panopticon gaze. 'I'm deeply fond of watercolours.'

It was as if she felt scared of reaching the actual reason for their visit. Her nerves drove her to talk, but to talk about nothing that mattered very much; something, in fact, that didn't matter at all – room decoration. Mart thought he could guess what brought them.

'Watercolours, so unvulgar, so unbrash, so gently declaring "pray take me as I am",' she said, 'so true to the moment when the artist spotted his/her topic and set up her/his easel and began. And don't let anyone claim that watercolours are easier to do than oils. Water is . . . well, watery. It's liable to run and needs strict control. So, the watercolourist must have the inspirational element but also management skills or it'll be the day the damn dam broke. I suppose it could be argued that all

artistic production depends on such a fusion – you can't reproduce the almost magically created Chopin piece without the
mechanical ability to hit the right notes with the right emphases
and timing – but the water in watercolours demands special
aquatic busybodying. Think of that inscription asked for by
Keats to go on his gravestone: "Here lies one whose name was
writ in water," meaning insubstantial.

'My mother was in many ways an arrantly stupid cow but
she often correctly pointed out that "water always finds its own
level"; and that level is downwards as far as it can get, including
through gaps in the floorboards. Thus, a watercolour artist has
a continuous problem in keeping the water from slipping down
her/his legs to the ground.'

Roy said, 'Mothers, despite themselves, can come up with
all sorts. I remember a—'

'Then, the room has, too, its armchairs and settee in uncut
moquette, infinitely serviceable, an irresistible invitation to
relax,' Flora replied. 'Whether *cut* moquette as against uncut
would have the same happy effect has to remain moot. We have
no example here. I stick to the "settee" name though some find
it low-class – probably because it's bracketed with other somewhat snootily regarded nouns, such as "serviette", "kitchenette".
It's that "ette" sound. People seem to think it's from the French
and fusspotty. But why take against French? Those who would
outlaw "settee" tend to prefer "sofa". Well "sofa" is from Arabic
and therefore just as much a foreign import as any "ette" word.
In fact, "settee" isn't foreign at all, but a development from
the old English "settle" – meaning a place to sit, which is,
obviously, what a settee is, even in this twenty-first century.'

'Can I offer you both a glass of sherry,' Mart said, 'speaking
of matters continental? Tesco's own.' He went to the sideboard
for a tray, the bottle and three glasses. Flora was in one of the
armchairs. Roy settled on the settle-settee-sofa. Moss served
the wine, then sat down in another of the armchairs.

'Are you sure we're not imposing on you?' Flora said, sipping.

'I imagine you can intuit why we've come,' Roy said, 'and
why we'd prefer to talk here rather than at Sedge.'

'Flora mentioned a changed atmosphere there,' Mart said.
'Probably this is in the nature of universities, in fact of many

kinds of organisation – a dynamism, an urge to improve and
go on improving. A university must constantly move forward,
otherwise, atrophy and collapse.'

'It's no fucking improvement,' Flora said. The gushing
preliminaries and lavishly decorous admiration of the room's
pictures and furniture had obviously been ditched, at last.

'This is a little embarrassing,' Roy said.

'In which way?' Moss asked, though he thought he was
beginning to understand which way.

'You're part of it, aren't you, Mart?' Flora said.

'Of what?'

'Of the change at Sedge,' Flora said. 'You're one of them.'

'One of what?' Mart said.

'Changes,' Flora replied.

'But we're not here to blame you,' Roy said. 'That's not at
all in our remit. We look upon you, Mart, as—'

'We want to get things into the open,' Flora said. 'There are
decisions to be made.'

'We don't consider you the instigator, Mart. You went along.
It could be argued you had no real choice.'

'Of what?' Moss replied.

'It all began as a totally unplanned incident, didn't it?' Roy
said.

'Which?'

'No evidence of devious scheming.' Moss thought he might
be getting hard cop–soft cop treatment. Roy said. 'How *could*
it have been planned? True, Rowena's supping-up tendency is
well-known, but the way things went at the inaugural was utterly
unpredictable. Rowena, pissed again, falls asleep. You are
shocked but continue, bravely unperturbed, and in due course
wake her and win her fascination by recounting what the
gamekeeper was giving her ladyship and where. Lawford is
unstintingly grateful. Perhaps his own sex life gets a lift and a
happy variant or two because of your lecture. At any rate, you're
suddenly the inadvertent golden boy, Mart. Most probably you'll
get a top-table invite to Standfast Fort for the Plain Parlour
centenary banquet.

'That's perfectly all right. Indeed, it's better than all right.
Excellent. Lawford sees someone new, of unexpected talents,

and wants to avail himself of them. This, surely, can be only a plus, not just for Lawford but for Sedge. It would torpedo an unpleasant belief held by some that the principal is surrounded and propped up by an exclusive cabal or clique – Flora, myself and a couple of others that we needn't name now. On the contrary, Chote has shown himself willing to take support from wherever it comes. There is a transparency and welcome width to his behaviour. And when I say welcome I mean welcomed by all who have the health of Sedge prominent in their minds, including those like Flora and myself, supposedly members of the specially favoured, self-protecting, narrow cluster.'

'Roy is right, up to a point,' Flora stated. 'Naturally, anyone who strengthens Lawford strengthens Sedge and is a boon. Boons are much needed. But there can be side effects – very hurtful, negative side effects. It's because Roy and I came to realize this – independently of each other at first – yes, it's because of this realization that we decided we must talk in confidence, away from the Sedge buildings, to you, Mart. I've mentioned the very deplorable change of atmosphere at Sedge. But I wonder whether you, in fact, are conscious of this, even though you are there as often as Roy and myself. To you, things might seem all tickety-boo: any changes are good changes, making things better than you have ever known them because what Roy and I would see as a darkening, a falling away, you, Mart, might regard as blissful sunshine and triumph. You're suddenly *in* with L. Chote, a success.'

She sipped. 'Potentially, you're our sodding ruin, Moss, or you'd like to be. You sit on your naff, bourgeois furniture, surrounded by wanked-out daubs on the walls, untroubled, snug, smug, while Roy and I are made to feel obsolete, discarded, useless, even traitorous. Yes, that. If you're such a sex guru, why are you here on your own when we call without fore-warning? OK, you're divorced from Grace. Don't you have any replacements? And then the sherry? Are we at an Oxbridge tutorial, for God's sake? Do this banal room and your inaugural performance about brisk and saucy coitus, satisfy you now?'

'Well, Flora, I don't think much of that's particularly to the point,' Roy said.

'Doesn't it make you enraged to see such grotesque

contentment while we are victimized?' Flora replied. Moss
guessed she'd be about fifty. She was middle height, her eyes
very pale blue and friendly even while she tore into him and
his sitting room. She had a very hearty, unapologetic way of
saying 'fucking' and 'sodding', and gave the 'f' and the 'uck'
and the 'dd' sounds full wham. This differed from routine
cursing: her heart was in it, though her face remained kindly
and apparently eager for eternal matiness. There were certain
words that Moss liked to mess about with. 'Dichotomy' was
one, meaning a difference, a division where one might have
expected a unity. If they ever brought in a Nobel prize for
dichotomy, Flora would walk away with it: genial, carer's
appearance; moody, switchback soul.

Mart considered it would be wrong and cliché-driven to
describe her features as mobile. They weren't. They never moved
away from expressing total amiability, and this accompanied the
initial doorstep civilities just now and the multi-layered contempt
she'd directed at Martin and his uncut moquette redoubt. She
had on a heavy dark brown duffel coat, untoggled while indoors,
over a vividly striped – scarlet, yellow, purple – high-necked
blouse and bell-bottom black trousers. Her feet were small in
pink, very high-heeled and sharply pointed shoes.

'Think of dear Roy,' she said. 'For at least months and
possibly years he has brown-nosed Chote with unwavering
diligence and, indeed, relish. You won't find anyone in Sedge
who can put as much sincerity and approval into the word
"certainly".

'The principal will say something – quite possibly something
virtually lunatic – and Roy, with a fine, discriminating smile
will reply, "Certainly". He doesn't overdo this in case it starts
to sound like mockery. No, he'll adjust with seamless skill to
a resounding, "Absolutely", in support of some other blatant
Chote crap. There is a benign, Darwinian strategy from Roy
here; although Lawford Chote is frequently wrong and farcical
he is sometimes right, and right about big, brave, admirably
creative proposals for Sedge. Roy has decided that Chote's
plentiful barmy ideas and behaviour must be approved so that
the principal's confidence remains intact, enabling him occasionally to produce one of these splendid, unique, seminal

developments for the university. Roy doesn't fling such endorsements around willy-nilly. They are specifically crafted for use on Lawford Chote, like a made-to-measure suit. Is Lawf aware of it – the brilliant accuracy and thoroughly simulated affection that's gone into this generous kowtowing? Perhaps he *was* once and felt grateful. But now? Roy is cast off, as I, too, am cast off. Why? Because some shallow, flashy, smarmy bastard comes along and uses these slimy qualities to get the approval of the principal's boozed-as-buggery wife and, through her, Lawford Chote's approval, too. You, Moss.'

Roy Gormand began to weep. It was noisy theatrical, unignorable weeping, not controlled, manly, muted grief but recurrent great waves of sobbing accompanied by fitful arm waving. It seemed wrong for someone on an uncut moquette settee or sofa. Mart's house stood in a fairly modern terrace. The walls were not thick and solid as in older style properties and he felt afraid neighbours might hear this heartbroken din and wonder whether something terrible had happened or was happening to him. Flora and Roy had come in Flora's Ford and it stood out front. That might cause people next door – on either side – to suppose a visitor or visitors had brought stress or tragedy to Mart's place, say forcible debt collection or a gangland revenge. He didn't want them thinking he was a crybaby.

Roy had his sherry glass, still half full, in one hand. He stared down at it and then at some indeterminate spot on one of the walls, then back to the glass. It reminded Martin of the way place kickers in rugby went through their ritual: first a glance at the angled ball on the ground; then a longer look at the goal posts; then the attempt to send the ball over the crossbar. Roy seemed about to fling the glass and the sherry to shatter on the selected area of plaster as part of his roaring sorrow display.

Flora obviously interpreted things the same. She stood quickly, feinted with her right and then switched stance to punch Roy hard with her left on his right cheekbone, just below the eye, a classic straight jab, not a haymaker or upper-cut. Although Roy didn't fall, the blow forced his head around sharply twenty degrees to the right, but Moss thought there'd be no bone splintering. He wondered whether Flora had dealt with him like this at other times of crisis. Mart tried to remember if he had ever

seen Roy around the Sedge corridors with abrasions to his face
and/or teeth missing. The punch seemed very precisely and
knowingly placed so that it would destabilize and bring pain
but not knock him out or require surgery. 'Calm yourself, Roy,
would you, please, you showy, waistcoated, near-defunct git?'
she purred. 'We both feel for you, I'm sure, but this sympathy
has boundaries and you'd better recognize them. Blub away if
you like. A blub is commensurate with the hurt Chote has caused
you. But no vandalising.' She took the glass from him. He did
not resist.

He had been sitting crouched slightly forward on the settee,
but now moved himself back and straightened, as if this consti-
tuted part of a recovery. It was like coming to attention while
seated, possibly a drill he'd learned when called up in World
War Two. He wiped his eyes with the backs of his hands. He
was near retirement age – mid-sixties – with plentiful grey-white
hair, nicely cut. He had a square face with brown eyes behind
thin-framed glasses, a deep unlined brow, upper mouth false
teeth, too white and too immaculately shaped. He was short-
legged but stretched out his paces when on his feet, possibly
hoping people would think he must be taller, to cover so much
ground at one pop.

He wore a three-piece, grey double-breasted suit, the jacket
unbuttoned now, the edge of a spectacle case poking out from
one of the waistcoat pockets. His lips were full. Mart wondered
whether they'd plumped themselves out like that through
framing so many concurring, unctuous, comfortable phrases for
Lawford. It was hard to think of lips like those saying anything
cantankerous or niggardly. Roy's job title made him sound
important (Sedge Developments Director) but he had only very
minor power; Chote looked after most of that area himself,
'Development is my life-theme,' he'd said in an article written
for the *Sedge News* quarterly magazine.

'As you can see, Martin, it's an emotional matter for me.
Flora is younger, so although it is an emotional matter for her,
too, it is also a very practical matter. Does she want to stay on
at Sedge in these changed, shaming conditions, or does she
look for a post elsewhere? Also, for me, a room is just a room,
so I don't feel the rage that Flora obviously does. For her, this

room betokens your selfishness, your indifference to the appalling indignity Lawford has imposed on both of us, and perhaps on Carl Medlicott, also. I'll be gone soon. I don't have to think of a tomorrow and a string of tomorrows here. It's the past I think of, Mart, and my loyalty to him and his cause, all of that now apparently disregarded, spurned.' Gormand seemed about to start sobbing again and slumped a little on the settee. The right cheekbone had a red-black swelling, but Moss felt certain now that the bone was intact.

'Unfailing devotion came from Ray to Chote,' Flora stated. 'This was sucking-up of a quality rarely encountered among educated adults; connivance of an unparalleled purity and enthusiasm. Now, as poor Roy remarks, this wholesome relationship is abruptly and permanently expunged, blotted out.'

Gormand said, 'For instance we hear that Lawford asked for a schedule of our timetable on a specific day and a specific time. The reasons are not clear. Whatever they might be, though, it is unpleasant, chilling, to think we have been spied upon. To what purpose, Mart? Flora's guess is that it's something to do with a photograph she's been informed of by an acquaintance at the U.F.C., a photo of you and Lawford in his official Volvo seemingly on a sightseeing tour around Charter. Flora's U.F.C. pal says that about you there was a—'

'*I* can report what she said, thank you, Roy,' Flora replied. 'Rest while you recover. She reported noting a "complicit" appearance on your face, Mart.'

'What does it look like, a complicit face?' Moss asked.

'Complicit,' Flora replied.

'There wasn't much to be complicit *in,* was there?' Mart said.

'Was there?' Flora said.

'A seemingly innocent little journey but to what purpose?' Roy asked. 'You'll have seen Charter Mill frequently in your goings and comings about the city.'

'And we are not the only ones curious about that journeying, are we?' Flora said.

'Lawford didn't know the photographs were going to be taken,' Moss said.

'Of course he didn't know they were going to be taken. His

expedition to Charter had been turned against him, trumped, hadn't it?' Flora said.

'Had it?' Mart replied.

'Despite all his damn slyness he's rumbled,' Flora said. 'Or not just Chote, you as well, Mart. Let me give you the full scene, will you?'

'Which scene?' Moss said.

'The scene as Flora sees it,' Roy said. He seemed pretty well OK now after the punch and talked clearly. He bent and picked up his glass from near his feet, where Flora had put it, and took a drink to help. 'And, generally speaking, the same as I see it,' he added.

'U.F.C. have not only a copy of the photo but the date and time it was taken,' Flora said. 'This would indicate, I think, that it comes from someone in Charter, someone who knew about the filming. As I'd expected, the date and time match the dates and times of Chote's timetabling inquiries, Mart. This confirms that he wanted to know whether one of us, or more than one, might have been around to witness your start in the pictured Volvo – to witness it and to make a call to Tane, or one of Tane's people, to say you were on your combined way.

'So, you'll reply that nobody watching that departure would know where Chote was taking you. This is a naïve reaction though, isn't it? What we can see is that at the Charter end they instantly and rightly assume the Volvo is coming there, and, accordingly, get the camera man or woman into position. I say "instantly" because they wouldn't have much time to arrange for the filming. It's only a couple of miles from Sedge. I say "instantly" for another reason, too. The reaction to that tip-off at Charter is virtually automatic and instinctive. Doesn't it look as if someone there – possibly Tane himself, perhaps one of his team – hear in the call from Sedge that with Chote in the car is someone not normally considered as one of Lawford's particular mates – Roy, me, Carl Medlicott. The swift Charter deduction is that Chote has a new lieutenant and wants to break him in, show him the likely objective in Lawf's colonising dream? The fact that you knew already what Charter Mill looked like is not important to Lawford. He wants you, Mart, to see those buildings and playing fields in a different fashion from previously, see them as an apprentice conquistador might – as a possible prize, as a target.

'Now, as a matter of fact, Roy and I would agree with that assessment of events. You are the new man, Moss. Roy and I are nowhere. That's how he and I might read the situation. Not, though, how Chote does. He believes Roy, Carl and I were not nowhere but very much *some*where – somewhere that enabled one of us, maybe more than one, to watch the Volvo and its passenger hit the road and let Charter know about it. Hence the research into our timetables. He's hunting for a traitor, traitors. Can any of us – Roy, Carl, I – ever work properly with him again after this disgusting slur?'

'If that disgusting slur really does exist, Flora,' Gormand said.

'Of course it exists, you limp oaf,' Flora replied. 'That's what we're here to confirm, Mart. If it's the case, I'm putting myself on the market for a job somewhere else. Possibly even with Tane. This ludicrous behaviour from Chote almost certainly means he hasn't got the kind of brain and stamina that might save Sedge. I'm not going down with the ship. Lawford can, if he wants to. He's the captain, isn't he? Captains do.'

'It wasn't you who rang Charter about the Volvo was it, Flora?' Roy asked.

'Who says anybody rang?' she replied.

'Well, I thought that was your theory,' Roy said.

'Yes, Flora,' Moss said.

'Am I reading the situation right, Mart?' Flora asked.

'I had a ride out to Charter with Lawford Chote, yes,' Moss said. 'The purpose I'm not sure about.' Moss tried to give this a brush-off tone.

It didn't work. '*I'm* sure,' Flora said. Apart from that minor emphasis on the 'I'm' Flora spoke more or less off-handedly, as if Mart's opinion didn't rate. She obviously believed almost everybody would expect her to see and understand matters better than anyone else; and therefore she didn't need to bluster and/or harangue.

'As I mentioned earlier, the thing about Flora is she cuts through to the very core of things,' Roy said.

'Does she?' Mart replied.

Yes, Moss could accept that she often did. The Volvo

hop-over to Charter had probably been what Flora said: a kind
of recruitment device by Lawford to bring Mart into the topmost
Chote team, a brief, motorized induction ceremony. But,
although that's what might have been in Chote's mind, Moss
detested this interpretation of the Charter Mill excursion. He
didn't want to be regarded as a principal's stooge, a principal's
yes-man, his minion. It had always depressed him to observe
how Roy and some of the others in Chote's retinue would
slavishly agree with him, defer to him, creep to him. Mart hoped
he had a more independent spirit than that and what he'd heard
described as 'proper pride' – not vanity, not coxcombery, but
decently earned, solid self-esteem. He wouldn't allow Flora's
poisonous caricature of him to kill that.

Mart could understand how someone in a leadership position
like Lawford might get excited and energized about possibly
extending the scope of that leadership, conferring his unique
skills and strength on new areas; more or less an obligation.
Moss had mentioned atrophy and collapse to Flora just now
– the penalties for failing to move forward. Moss didn't know
much about capitalism but he had often heard that a business
could not stand still. It had to develop or it would be overtaken
and crushed by competitors. Same with some public bodies,
such as universities? Chote wanted to do the overtaking, not
drop behind. Moss regarded this as a reasonable ambition, in
fact, a fine, necessary ambition and didn't mind helping Lawford
with it, if Mart could.

And he didn't mind having traipsed over to Charter with
Lawford to share a reminder of where, if Chote managed matters
OK, the Sedge expansion would take place; this was part of
that excitement and energy. But to sympathise didn't mean Mart
had become Roy Mark Two, he hoped, or would ever become
Roy Mark Two, gutted and lickspittling.

'Who chose them?' Flora asked.

'Chose what?' Mart said.

'The watercolours,' she said. 'I imagine it must have been
Grace. *You* wouldn't pick such tame, insipid stuff. And not even
she wanted them when you split, I guess. You hang on to them
out of a quaint sense of loyalty, I suppose?'

'No, definitely not Grace. *I* picked them,' Moss replied.

Actually, Flora was right again and Grace *had* chosen them, then lost interest. But Mart felt he must do a bit of self-assertion on Flora. He didn't mean to answer her questions about Chote's and his own aims and intentions. 'I love the watercolours,' he said. 'Gentle, unobtrusive yet amazingly alive, so intent on their unique, individual identities.'

'What the fuck does that mean?' Flora replied.

Exactly. He didn't say it, though. He found the pictures wishy-washy and lackadaisical and had several times considered taking them down and dumping them on the Salvation Army for one of their raffles. But that would entail buying other works of about the same size so as to cover the faded patches of wallpaper where the watercolours had hung; or getting the room redecorated. He couldn't be arsed.

FIFTEEN

2014

Mart Moss said, 'At some time reasonably soon the committee will have to go as a body to look at prospective sites for the statues. You'll note I say "sites", not "site", and perhaps you'll also note that I say it tentatively, a slight tinge of query in my voice. But, just the same, I believe I have it right. Despite the suggestion in a previous session that the two figures should share one plinth, and, therefore, obviously, one site, though moveable, I felt that the discussion of that proposal – albeit a thorough, balanced and sensitive discussion – yes, I felt nonetheless that the majority view quite perceptibly favoured separate plinths, and, as a probable consequence, separate sites on the two campuses, giving each statue its own personal, psychologically speaking, autonomous space.

'If anyone feels I have misread the committee's thinking on this, I would, of course, be willing to put the matter to a vote, on the simple question: "Do you favour a unitary plinth per statue or one binary plinth per paired statues?" – abstentions to rate as acceptance of the *status quo,* the *status quo* being the original working assumption of one statue one plinth.'

Wayne Ollam (Philosophy) said, 'No need, Mart, none at all. I think you've caught the general view accurately. That is, respectful, positive consideration of the solo plinth with double occupancy suggestion, but eventual abandonment of that idea as over-complicated, particularly the inescapable, endless requirement to transport the duo and their close-cohabited plinth across the city at specified intervals. If the statues were visible on the back of a lorry during such trips the general public, although quite unbiased, might feel this arrangement to be laborious, contrived and even slightly farcical. On the other hand, were the plinthed couple moved between locations secretly – say under tarpaulin on the lorry, or in the windowless back of a van, and this became known to the media, we could be knocked, mocked, for behaving sneakily and furtively with the images of two men who, in their time, had stood for transparency, openness, honesty – fundamental qualities of universities worldwide. Also, because of this periodic transfer, requiring time on the road between Sedge and Charter, or, to put it another way, for the sake of equality, Charter and Sedge, there would inevitably be spells when both campuses had no statue or statues at all. Agreed, that might be only a brief break since the distance is not great, but I believe we should strive to establish a completely uninterrupted continuum, symbolic of a steady, strong, unthreatened future for the new, composite Sedge.'

Theo Bastrolle (Business Studies) said, 'And if the statues were single-plinthed and swapped around at set intervals between the two campuses, Sedge and Charter, or Charter, Sedge, like changes of shift, it would similarly look – what were Wayne's words – look, yes, laborious and contrived. There's another demeaning comparison, isn't there: one of those barometers where two figurines came out in turns according to what the air pressure and weather are doing?'

'So, if Victor and Lawford, or Lawford and Victor, are to be mono-plinthed and fixed in their respective locations we come back to the major problem touched on at a previous meeting of who is where?' Lucy Lane (History) said. 'I recognize that the statues could be close to each other, without that implying they're at each end of the same plinth. We have already considered proximity issues such as the height disparity between dumpy Chote and beanpole Tane, or beanpole Tane and dumpy Chote.

'But if there were to be proximity, though not on a single plinth, it would imply that only one of the campuses would get the statues and the high board might not see this as suitable. There would be an acute risk of false appearance. For instance, if both were installed near each other in what used to be Charter, this might be interpreted by some as meaning that they jointly brought the new university into happy conjunction with the older one; whereas it's clear to anyone who reads even the smallest amount of documentation and press coverage of the period that Lawford Chote loathed the notion of a merger, regarded it as a kind of slumming to have any link with Charter, let alone a formal marriage. On the other hand, if both individually plinthed statues were set down not far from each other in the Sedge campus it could be taken as a statement that Lawford had gladly welcomed Vic Tane into his bailiwick as an admired, supportive partner which, of course, is top-of-the-range bollocks.'

Angela Drape (Environmental Engineering) said, 'Had we been thinking of statue placements in 1987 we'd have met no real difficulty. Lawford Chote was installed at Sedge and Victor Tane at Charter Mill, or to put it differently, Victor Tane at Charter Mill, Lawford Chote at Sedge. But, clearly, the problems wouldn't have arisen then because they were both alive, not requiring statues, and actually in their obvious *situs*. Do we now, a quarter of a century later, follow that pattern and put the Tane statue at what is today the Charter Mill campus of Sedge and the Chote statue in what is today the Sedge campus of Sedge University, a title which encompasses both?'

'What this comes down to ultimately, I think,' Elvira Barton (Classics) said, with a let's-cut-the-crap rasp, 'is whether one of the apparent options presenting themselves to us for selection is in truth an option at all. We would never choose it. I refer, of course, to the notion that in the disposition of statues Lawford Chote's could conceivably be allocated to Charter, while Tane's at Sedge is a perfectly feasible concept since he became Principal of the merged Charter and Sedge, or Sedge and Charter. Consequently, he's entitled to be at either site; and – specifically – is entitled to what some might regard as the more prominent, city centre display. There is no such similar obviousness in a suggestion that Lawford Chote's replica should go to Charter. There would be something crazy in any decision to send the Chote image there. Some would put things much stronger than that and possibly talk of Lawford's being dumped out there – "out there" referring to its semi-rural, semi-obscure setting – as a kind of punishment for his mismanagement and presumptuousness, a kind of malign, sneering joke.'

'Like Devils' Island or Alcatraz or Siberia,' Bill Davey (French) said.

'In what sense a joke, Elvira?' Gordon Upp (Linguistics) asked.

'There are still people around – me, for instance – who have heard that it had been Chote's blatant boast that he and Sedge would take over what was then regarded as the lesser, entirely undistinguished institution, Charter Mill,' Elvira said. 'He would probably have gone about slagging off this neighbour for needing a name that blared possession of a charter in order to call itself a university. This, he would have argued, showed it was very shaky – and deservedly so – about its identity and status. Was Oxford or Harvard or the Sorbonne ever mistaken for something other than universities because they didn't have charter or the French equivalent in their titles?

'But then comes the reversal, the cruel, absolute, humiliating reversal and an end to Lawford's braggadocio. Sedge doesn't eat up Charter because Sedge is broke and can't afford that kind of delicacy. Instead, Charter makes a snack of Sedge and spits Lawford out like a lump of irredeemable gristle. To put his statue at the former Charter now would be like saying to him, "You wanted Charter Mill, didn't you? Now you've got it, but only a tolerated bit as big as your plinth, Chotey. Look about you and see the quiet orderliness and solvency that brought Sedge last-minute salvation, but brought it at a cost." If the statue's face showed the authentic Lawford self-satisfaction and arrogance, it would come across, wouldn't it, as an indication of outright madness, as if he couldn't realize what a terminal mess he'd made of things; still imagined he had a future and was on his way to a knighthood or even a peerage for services to higher education. We surely can't allow such gross lampooning of someone who had several genuine achievements in his career. Well, one or two.'

'I think we shouldn't make our minds up until we've done an organized, on-the-spot examination of each potential site, whether in what was Charter Mill or the original Sedge,' Mart Moss said. 'The actuality can be a brilliant help in attaining clarity of vision when things are complex and clouded.'

'Of course, Mart, you would most likely be able to endorse that from your own experience, wouldn't you?' Claud Nelmes (Physics) said.

'Not sure I follow that, Claud,' Moss replied, in fact following it very well. He didn't fancy getting frogmarched into that snippet of history, though.

'I was a research student at Sedge during those run-up months to the merger crisis. I remember, don't I, Mart, that there was a kerfuffle about a picture of you and Lawford in his belligerent Volvo apparently sizing up Charter as a possible target in a Sedge expansion scheme? A Chote expansion scheme. "Come in under my umbrella, Charter, and feel the instant benefit." It seemed both of you wanted to see that "actuality" you've just mentioned. Or re-see. This was the rumour around, anyway. And a copy of the photo reached the Education Ministry heavy mob in London, didn't it, leading to a series of clean-up interventions?'

'All sorts of rumours flying then weren't there, Claud?' Moss replied.

'But this seems to me an example of that actuality thing,' Nelmes said.

'Actuality *thing*?' Mart replied, as if amused.

'You spoke just now about actuality, Mart, referring to it as "a brilliant help" to our thinking and understanding. Contact with actuality, you seemed to say, would be an advance on what so far is only ideas – ideas in this case about the statue sites. You suggested, didn't you, that we should go "as a group" to see, to experience in that *actuality*, the competing emplacements.'

'Ah, we've got a very obvious touch of *esse est percipi* here,' Elvira snarled.

'Absolutely!' Lucy said.

'I've never seen a better case of *esse est percipi*,' Bill Davey said.

'A case of *what*?' Claud replied. 'We've got *what*?'

Of course, Mart had made this comparison himself when actually on the Volvo trip with Lawford, but he didn't say anything about that now and let Elvira give the explanation.

'Dr Johnson and his pal Boswell were talking after church one day about Bishop Berkeley's theory that things existed only in the mind – *esse est percipi* (to be is to be perceived),' she said. 'Boswell comments that, although this is blatant rubbish, to refute it might be difficult and perhaps impossible. Johnson lashes out with his boot and kicks a large stone, hurting his foot. "I refute it thus," he says, meaning that the stone had a real, an *actual*, existence, and had it before the kick, and would have it afterwards, not depending on someone's mind thinking about it.

'We, so far, here in our committee, are dealing in ideas – *only* ideas – regarding the statue sites, as Mart would appear to suggest. The statues don't yet exist. However, we have in our minds, certain abstract qualities that they will represent – commemoration, praise, gratitude. The significant phrase here is "in our minds". *Only* at this stage "in our minds". What Mart wants us to do is move forward to the next point – reality, the possible locations themselves.

'Mart would like us to get to the potential sites and perhaps not aim kicks at them but get the feel of the places where a statue, or the statues, might stand and note the nature of the ground under our feet – perhaps grass, perhaps cement, perhaps timber – and experiment with the kind of views available from such sites. This he considers will bring guidance and clarity to our deliberations, and I'm prepared to believe he is probably correct.'

'It would be rather illogical, wouldn't it, Elvira, for us to go about kicking stones given that the statues we have in our minds will most likely themselves be made of stone,' Jed Laver (Industrial Relations) said.

'Interesting,' Moss replied. 'Perhaps on that fascinating observation we should adjourn now.' He'd heard enough discussion of this topic and similar. The Volvo saunter had embodied all the vainglorious absurdities of Lawford's principalship, and Mart would prefer not to be associated with it now. He'd detected a *j'accuse* tone in Nelmes's voice when he asked about Martin's part in that reconnaissance operation with Chote, a reconnaissance that became irrelevant and fatuous almost as soon as it had taken place.

That minor travel episode turned out to be much less important than the series of journeys from London to Sedge that it provoked. In Whitehall, Geraldine Fallows – later *Baroness Fallows* – had learned of the sortie and seen the photograph. Result? Neddy Lane-Hinkton is sent down to vet the local black-pudding hash and to discover what the fuck is going on at Sedge, the first of many nosy, investigative deputies on mission from HQ. Unfortunate truths about the mess-up at Sedge began to emerge and, in a short while, imminent disintegration was diagnosed and emergency treatment begun: i.e., Lawford neutralized and virtually booted out, along the lines of Dr Johnson's treatment of Bishop Berkeley's idealism.

Martin recalled that he'd felt half sympathetic to Chote's aim to expand Sedge; but also half uneasy about his attempt to enlist Mart by getting him to think of Charter mainly – entirely? – as a desirable and available slab of real estate, lecture room, labs, a canteen, playing fields. Mart had often in those immediately pre-crisis days tried to picture what Chote was like as, simply, Lawford Chote; as just another man, not as head of Sedge. But Martin had found that, as far as he was permitted to see, Lawford lived for Sedge; or rather he lived for Sedge with Lawford Chote at the top of it and resolutely eager to be at the top of something akin but bigger. There were good aspects to this. He brought drive and a kind of creativity to Sedge – his kind. And his kind of creativity demanded a lot of money and some luck. At or near the end of his tenure neither of these was to hand.

Now, Moss wished he had been a good deal less than half in favour of Lawford's jinxed ambitions. Although that was only the wisdom of aftermath, it would have to do. It dictated his attitude to the Volvo-Charter-Sedge-Lawford-Moss situation today, and today was where Mart indubitably was at. 'Thank you all very much,' he said. 'Reassemble in a fortnight, same time.'

SIXTEEN

1987

'I wanted to congratulate you, Vic.'

In his office at Charter Mill, Victor Tane had a call on the confidential line from Geraldine Fallows at the Ministry's Universities Finance Centre in London. Her voice was steely, in the fashion that voices of executive rank in the Ministry's Universities Finance Centre in London generally were steely, but traces of excitement and faux warmth came over, too.

He'd been handwriting a substantial letter to his mother when the phone rang, describing what he regarded as interesting news about himself, underlining some crucial words, and exclamation marking several of the most startling, to give an ironic flavour. He got a real kick out of penning exclamation marks, which he'd found wasn't the case if he typed the letter on his computer. He felt that the narrow nib imprinting the paper like that was the culmination of a happy trek from his brain, where the decision to use that piece of punctuation was made, then down his arm and fingers and the body of the fountain pen to the very ready surface adjoining the word to be kitted out with the exclamation mark.

His mother had been dead for just over two years but he felt it wise to get in touch like this every few months or oftener. It amounted to more than an antidote to grief; had not much to do with grief at all. He would put his home address including postcode as sender on the back of the envelope and it soothed him thoroughly when the letter was returned with 'NOT KNOWN', or 'GONE AWAY' alongside the franked stamp, usually in pencil, and usually in capitals.

'GONE AWAY' was the inscription he preferred. The 'NOT KNOWN' response seemed an attempt to negate her, claim she didn't exist and never *had* existed. Because Tane knew this to be untrue, he deduced that the 'NOT KNOWN' statement showed nothing about his mother but proved that whoever had written this comment was possibly stupid or slapdash or indifferent. It troubled Victor. He felt that his mother might still be around and potentially active, although not known to some.

This disturbing factor was pleasingly absent from 'GONE AWAY'. He took these words to mean that there had certainly been someone of Tane's mother's name at this address but she had decided to change locations: had voluntarily removed herself from contact with the recipient, recipients, of the letter, and therefore from Tane's reckoning, also. He could confidently reassure himself that she wouldn't be turning up to yell at him in her customary style about the 'poncy uselessness' of his classics degrees, and then go systematically through his letter declaring every paragraph aimed at charming and updating her was shit.

He realized that the people now living at her last house would eventually get sick of returning his letters, and this could make him edgy, as if she must still be present somewhere and liable to accost him suddenly, the pages in her hand, most likely flecked with rage saliva. Or the folk at the receiving end might open the letter and read it, then write to tell him this one and most probably all those they'd sent back as 'NOT KNOWN' or 'GONE AWAY' were rot and full of daft dogs' cocks, as he knew exclamation marks were called in journalism.

'The photograph,' Geraldine said on the phone. 'Maybe I should have rung you earlier with my thanks, but I asked Neddy Lane-Hinkton to do a little prospecting at Sedge and wanted to get his account of things before I spoke to you.'

'Fluke,' Tane said.

'I don't believe in flukes. Some things are beyond our understanding, yes, but that doesn't make them flukes. Consider intuitions. Consider extra-sensory matters. There are more things in heaven and earth, Victor, than are dreamt of in your philosophy, as Hamlet almost says.'

'In this instance shouldn't that be "photography" not

"philosophy"?' Tane replied. He hated quotations, except those lifted from limericks on the walls of public lavatory cubicles. He knew thousands of quotations, English, French, Backslang, German, Latin, Greek, but would never use one, and suspected those who did. They needed something to prop up their own thoughts and ideas, so went and filched earlier versions of them, versions that had possibly endured for centuries and so must be strong and safe. *Hamlet* quotes he loathed above all. 'To be, or not to be, that is the question.' Most actors gave the 'that' a real wallop, as if to squash any other questions, especially banal queries such as 'do you take milk and sugar?' Well, perhaps to be or not to be *was* the fundamental question and most people decided to be rather than not to be just yet. Because of this they looked both ways before trying to cross the road. It was so obvious that it wasn't worth going on about. One quote from *Hamlet* Tane did treasure: 'Give it understanding, but no tongue', i.e., think, and keep your trap shut.

'Our Organized Crime And Its Defeat department here runs regular surveillance exercises and tests for students hoping to get into the police or security services,' he told Geraldine. 'We are very hands-on, as they say. One of them did traffic filming and happened to net the Volvo and its two occupants, along with many other vehicles. Nothing planned. A fluke. Gloria Sondial, department head and a sharp lady, skimming through the kid's work to check clarity, focus, composition, realized what we had and let me know about it.'

'That's hardly fluke, is it, Vic? The opposite: she saw the importance. She made a decision to tell you, show you. All very logical.'

'The filming – luck,' he replied.

'I prefer to think mysterious, subliminal hunch,' Geraldine said. 'I prefer to think unexplainable inspiration. Britain needs people like that student, and like Gloria, in MI5 and 6. There's something psychic about this revelatory sequence.'

'I agree that if Chote noticed the cameraman, he'll probably think Charter had been tipped off by phone from someone in Sedge that the Volvo had set out on its way to eyeball Charter, and I ordered the filming. I've heard Lawford can be a bit paranoid.'

'But how would anyone at Sedge know they were coming to you, even if they were spotted leaving?'

'Chote would probably reply, "There are more things in heaven and earth, Geraldine, than are dreamt of in your philosophy."'

'Look here, Vic, we're at a crux situation,' she replied.

'Crux how?' Tane asked.

'It's plain.'

'But how?'

'He was on a shopping excursion, wasn't he?'

'Chote?'

'Chote and his fresh chum.'

'Shopping in which way?'

'Your fucking way. Charter Mill way. I see it as a kind of plea, Vic.'

'See what?'

'The photograph. Or not simply the photograph, but the fact that you should send it to me.'

'It's not a fact. I didn't.'

'All right, all right, you didn't. I think I can work out why you wouldn't want to admit you did. You feel it might make you look weak, sneaky, unmanly. You wouldn't want to be deemed unmanly. You wouldn't want to be thought incapable of dealing with this yourself. I referred to a kind of plea, Vic. You'd probably feel ashamed to be caught making such a plea.'

'What plea?' Tane replied.

'This is the enemy at the gates, isn't it? I'm told we have recognisable bits of Charter in the picture's background. You smell danger. You smell intent. You smell machinations. This is Chote with a new lieutenant. Lawford no longer finds his usual top gang adequate. Forthcoming pressures will be too much for them. I've met some of this special caucus in previous dealings with Sedge, of course – Roy Gormand, Flora Ellison. Gormand at this sunset stage of his career is intellectually frail, feeble, merely a yes-man. I'm not sure he's ever been more than that. Now, he's liable to blub under stress, even negligible stress. Carl Medlicott, frequently unwell. Then Flora – subject to very disturbing mood swings, volatile, epically unreliable, unpredictable, no doubt a splendid, frantic shag if caught at the

juicy point in her emotional orbit, but Lawford needs something
else currently.

'This replacement, Martin Moss, unfledged in the Sedge-
Charter situation and possible – probable – future developments
seems to have impressed Lawford somehow. Well, I have a
notion how. Neddy did some nosing and comes up with a report
that Moss's inaugural as prof seemed to tickle Mrs Chote with
its commentary on Connie and the gamekeeper's romantic
variants. He decomatosed Rowena. You very prudently – if I
may say – very prudently see these changes – Gormand, Flora,
Medlicott out, Moss in – as an important indicator. It shows an
intensification of the Charter-Sedge tensions. Chote seeks to
increase his firepower. So, Martin Moss. Lawford will make
his gambit very soon.'

'Which gambit?'

'Lawford has the Sedge centenary celebrations coming up,'
Geraldine replied. 'He'll be feeling extremely bouncy, extremely
bullish and questing. You very prudently – again, if I may say
– very prudently decide to seek support from outside. Nothing
abject or craven in that, Vic. It's what we're here for. Hence I
get this copy of the photograph. A wholly unnecessary tact
means the snapshot is sent anonymously. But its message is
apparent. No caption is required, no disclosure of source. I'm
ringing now to ask you to let us know at once of any further
signs there that Chote or his new aide, Moss, might be contem-
plating other stratagems. Why I mentioned a crux, Victor. We
are very near something now.'

'Near what?' Tane said.

'I'm talking about signs that possibly only you in your
position would spot the underlying meaning of – or perhaps
with the intelligent help of someone like your gifted, clued-up
Gloria Sondial. To most folk the Volvo and its crew would
amount simply to a Volvo and its driver and passenger. It takes
unusual sensitivities and nous to get behind the obvious and
supply a context and a prognosis. I say once more, "Congratulations,
Vic," and please pass similar from me to Gloria.'

When she had rung off, Tane continued the letter to his
mother. 'As one of the items in "A Day Of Sport" put on by
the "Physical Education Sport And Bodily Wellbeing" (PESBW)

department here recently a seven mile walking race was featured
and it inevitably put me in mind of that sonnet you wrote about
a similar event. Do you recall it, dear Ma? I do, every line. But
you wrote so much poetry – including those longish parodies
of *Paradise Lost* books Five and Nine. Perhaps you forget some
of your other works. Let me then close with the aforementioned
sonnet. I recited it to some of the contestants after the competition. I don't think they liked it very much:

> TWO VIEWS OF THE WALKING RACE
> Preposterous goons, why must you jig and twitch
> like this, all elbows, knees and tortured hips,
> heel-toe, heel-toe, contorted, spit-slimed lips?
> You jerks reduce to robot jerks the rich
> refinements of the human frame; you've turned
> your bodies into rule-clamped, comic sites.
> Now, here's the ref, arrived to check the rights
> and wrongs of what he dubs your styles. 'I've learned
> to spot the cheats,' he says, 'sly runners who
> pretend to walk, but flap their arses, lift
> their feet too high, all discipline adrift.
> The sport's grand skills rest only with a few:
> between their buttocks stars could fix a pin,
> then race, while never puncturing the skin.'

I'll say farewell for now, mother. Your ever distant son, Vicky

SEVENTEEN

1987

But Tane's mother didn't hate *all* sports. Although she
despised that kind of walking style required in racing,
and abominated, too, televised tennis with its scuttling,
servile ballboys and girls, she adored soccer and especially
goalkeepers, 'solitary between sticks, like an unmelted sugar

cube in tongs,' as she thought of them. It was because of her fervent regard for goalkeepers that one of them came to have what Victor considered quite a notable influence on the Sedge-Charter Mill situation. This wasn't – couldn't be – instant. It evolved over several years, thanks to Mrs Tane.

She'd written a poem about these 'custodians' – heartfelt and full of unbridled praise; none of that towering irritability plain in *Two Views*. It began, 'Oh, goalkeeper, my goalkeeper,' and, as Tane remembered it, this note of excited, all-out reverence was maintained to the end. Several times she'd told Victor that Albert Camus, the great French philosopher and Nobel Prize winner used to be a goalie in a local Algerian team, 'before he started all his seminal stuff about the Absurd.' Mrs Tane believed that goalkeeping helped put him on to this kind of philosophy because there was something comically farcical – absurd, in fact – about the sight of a goalkeeper powerfully, unsparingly, flinging himself to one side when trying to block a penalty, but, as it turned out, the absolutely wrong side. Didn't this glaringly demonstrate that human effort was pointless in a cruelly malevolent world? Oh goalkeeper, my goalkeeper, how noble you might be at times, and how mercilessly exposed.

'Good goalkeepers have courage, agility and undaunted free-spirited self-hood,' his mother insisted, 'this last above all.' Any evidence of serfdom in sport or in life generally always nauseated her – the mad rules, as she regarded them, imposed on contestants in a walking race; the bent-double fetch-and-carry ballboys and girls forced to make themselves more or less invisible, crouched low against the net post between rallies, like dogs waiting to be let off the leash; Victor Tane's sickening subservience to the rigidities of Greek and Latin grammar. Music of all types disgusted her because at the composition stage it was 'just blob notes clinging pathetically to stave lines, resembling hopeless messages stuck by prisoners on the barbed wire, perimeter fence of a concentration camp.'

Tane's father had been a couple of decades older than Amy, Tane's mother, but in his early fifties had persuaded an amateur club near where they lived to let him play in goal for their Thirds so as to please his wife and get at least some of her esteem.

Although he bought goalkeeper-type mittens he was useless, but brave. In his first and final game, when he'd already let in four goals, he rushed out, attempting to scoop the ball away from the feet of the opposing centre forward, to prevent his hat-trick, got badly kicked in the head and went into a coma from which he never recovered. Amy had the words, 'In a league of his own' inscribed on the gravestone.

Several years ago, probably 1981, she had come to visit Tane shortly after his appointment as Principal. It was a Saturday and the Charter Mill soccer team were due to play a Sedge eleven in the afternoon on the Charter Mill ground. A vivid rivalry would be on show in the match because of the geographical nearness of the two universities and Tane decided he must attend as a spectator, to demonstrate solidarity and support. He'd guessed his mother might be keen to see the game and mentioned it when they arranged her visit on the phone. Amy brought white wellington boots and thick, grey socks in her holdall. Tane wore his heavy walking shoes.

Lawford Chote, also, had obviously decided this match was a meaningful occasion in the Sedge-Charter relationship and was on the touchline with what Tane took to be a couple of his male staff, maybe from that special fawning coterie Victor had heard rumours of. Poor sods, if they didn't like soccer. But, then, Chote might not, either. It was a duty attendance, perhaps. Same for Tane. He'd have to try to nick some of his mother's enthusiasm. The heavens declare the glory of goalkeepers. As the teams took their positions for kick-off she'd said, 'Burly and tall enough to close off some of the space, admittedly.'

'Who?'

'The Sedge goalkeeper.' she said. 'But burliness and tallness are not necessarily enough.'

'Oh?' Victor replied.

'Although yours – Charter's – himself has some burliness and height, I can read something else there. Let's call it "inherent purpose", shall we, Vicky?'

'What inherent purpose?'

'Goalkeeping.'

'Surely the Sedge goalkeeper would also have that purpose, Ma? It's what goalkeepers do – keep goal.'

'Not the same,' she replied. 'But I wouldn't expect someone like you to appreciate this.'

'Someone like me in which respect?'

It had been a fine, cold November afternoon with a mild wind favouring Charter in the first half. There was no seating but a crowd of a couple of hundred, mostly undergraduates, stood around the touchlines, partisan, and noisy.

'It's a destiny, Victor.'

'What?'

'Goalkeeping. Not some drab job at the back given to someone just because of bulk and tallness to help him cope. No, a mission. A disposition. A designated role. A congenital urge. These are the in-built qualities the true goalkeeper has and they are immediately apparent to some of us.'

'Designated who by?' Victor asked.

'By blood, by fate. He has been singled out. He does not wear the striped, buttoned shirt like his ten colleagues but a single-colour, polo-necked jersey. In the Charter case, green. But you'll protest and say the Sedge goalkeeper also has a single-colour sweater, but purple. I don't argue that the distinctive top garment is the *only* exceptional factor. In some instances – such as Charter-man – it is the accompaniment, the, as it were, frame for all those other required factors.'

'Surely, Mother, the goalkeeper wears the heavier garment because this is a winter game and he might be required to stand around doing nothing much and therefore liable to get cold. His mittens would protect only very small areas. The mono-colour of the sweater-jersey isn't really of much relevance.'

She'd clearly found this ridiculously naive and had a good-natured, throaty chuckle at it. Then she said, 'Gabby twat.' She wore a double breasted black leather greatcoat which she'd told Tane was of the type used by Swedish army dispatch riders, a grey woollen scarf, tied like a running bowline knot, a navy bobble hat, also woollen, and brown corduroy trousers tucked into the socks and wellingtons.

Charter had made an easy task of drubbing Sedge, as Tane would have expected. After all, Charter had a Physical Education and Bodily Wellbeing degree course. It attracted students who, when they finished, might have a professional interest in sport, and so they devoted most of their university time to preparing themselves for that – skills, fitness, diet, psychology.

But the Sedge team would regard games as merely something aside from their serious work – a break, a relaxation. Charter beat them 6-0, four of the goals in the second half, as though Charter wanted to prove they could triumph just as well against the wind as with it. Psychology. Self-belief. Adaptability. The Charter goalkeeper had only two saves to make throughout, both simple and soft. But Amy Tate yelled 'Sublime!' when he made the first of them and 'Rapturous!' for the second. Tane, scared of seeming indifferent and/or churlish cried 'Bravo!' for each, with credible, robust power.

'I thought "Bravo!" was what opera groupies shouted,' his mother said.

After the final whistle, Chote and his mini-entourage had crossed the field and approached Amy and Victor in genial, brisk style. Tane introduced his mother and Chote introduced his companions, Carl Medlicott and Roy Gormand.

Chote said, 'We must congratulate you, Victor, on a fine win.'

'Yes, indeed,' Gorman said. 'Fine.'

'Deserved,' Medlicott said.

'Oh, certainly,' Chote said.

'Unquestionably,' Gormand said.

'You can see why he's called Victor,' Amy said.

'Indeed, indeed,' Gormand said with a thorough smile.

Tane could tell that his mother was almost into one of her wraths. A Swedish army dispatch rider wearing that type of coat to combat Scandinavian weather would reach his/her destination and hand over the dispatch without any knowledge of its contents or any opinions about the message. Mrs Tane, although in the same kind of coat, was different. She had attitudes, views.

She said, 'You three are totally content to see your lads conclusively squashed. Your words sound gracious and larded with fair's-fairness – gentlemanly, bourgeois, upper-crust English civility – but really it's because you don't give a fish's tit about the game. Victory or defeat are the same for you since in your reckoning a soccer match is but a soccer match, of no significance alongside all the academic, intellectual distinction you believe exists in Sedge. You speak *de haut en bas* and can afford to gush the compliments, patronize Victor and Charter with worthless praise.'

'There'd be no point in denying Charter were the better side, Mrs Tane,' Chote replied.

'That was patent,' Medlicott said. 'Our team strove, and strove, but, as Lawford stated, their striving fell short.'

'Unfortunately,' Gormand said.

'Your goalkeeper, dismally ungifted,' Amy Tane replied. 'A big lump of a journeyman, no extra-terrestrial glow.'

'My mother has made a study of goalkeeping,' Tane said, 'the inner qualities needed, not just the obvious ones.'

'This little area of ground behind him or her and immediately ahead is his or hers to patrol, to guard, to launch a counter attack from. If he, she, fails at this she, he is a nonentity, in your case a purple nonentity.'

Later, when the teams had showered and come together for a drink in the pavilion before their meal, Amy had made a path for herself to the Charter goal-keeper to tell him face-to-face how splendidly he performed his designated role and responded to his congenital urge. Tane went with her, but she did the talking. 'And your name?' she said. 'We shall want to follow your golden career. You will be getting many a fan letter from me via whichever top club the media report you as playing for – and I'm sure you *will* make it to a top club. ' His name was Bernard Optor. She handed lipstick for him to autograph the outer surface of one of her wellington boots.

And Amy did follow his career, presumably sent fan letters, and kept the signed boot dry. A couple of years later she had phoned Tane at home to ask if he'd seen the back page of the *Daily Mail*. He hadn't so she read a couple of sentences to him. They said that goalkeeper Bernie Optor had just signed a contract with one of the most famous Spanish sides that would bring him £140,000 a week, beside what he might earn from internationals.

And now, today, the phone rang once more, in his office this time. 'Principal? It's Bernard.' He pronounced it in the American way, Ber*nard,* probably as someone now rather cosmopolitan. 'How's Mrs Tane? Look, I hear a situation has developed there, what with tensions over the future for Charter and Sedge. Charter *or* Sedge. And I wonder if Sedge might be getting ahead on that. We ought to do something. I can't have my *alma mater* going to the wall.'

'What kind of thing, Bernard?'

'Yes, we ought to do something. After all, Principal, we beat them easily enough back whenever it was that afternoon, '81 was it? My final year. And I bet Charter have beaten them every year since. In that game – yes, '81 – I had hardly anything to do and I got almost paralysingly cold.'

'But you had the green jersey on and black mittens.'

'I have to work harder where I am now, I can tell you, Prince.'

EIGHTEEN

2014

Gordon Upp (Linguistics) said, 'What we have here, of course, is a process – the process of arranging, selecting the kind of statues we wish to recommend and their sites or site. Think of the Duke of Norfolk preparing the pageantry for a coronation or Royal wedding. But, also, our statue deliberations are a process that, as it were, looks at itself. It is reflexive.'

'Oh?' Theo Bastrolle (Business Studies) said. Instantly, Martin Moss recognized this 'Oh?' as, in fact, very much a Business Studies 'Oh?' – the kind of 'Oh?' that students in Theo's department would be taught for use in their commercial careers after graduating. For instance, the 'Oh?' should be their response to a sterling, euro or dollar figure demanded from them in some big-time company negotiations for bonds or commodities or easements. It was intended to express shock, disbelief, outrage at the preposterous, rip-off amount asked for. It suggested that the other party should think again and quote a charge not entirely unrelated to the one already cited but divided by two.

This 'Oh?'when uttered as a haggling ploy, said in coded, abbreviated form, 'Cheap! – at half the price.' Theo's 'Oh?' now didn't exactly match that situation, but it contained a similar unwillingness to accept meekly what he'd heard. In this exchange Moss thought the 'Oh?' from Theo might have a slightly different coded, abbreviated form, such as: 'What the fuck does "reflexive" mean?'

But Lucy Lane seemed to have grasped instantly what Upp's 'reflexive' signified. 'Clearly, Gordon,' she said. She was viewing with concentration and affection something in her hand-kerchief, like a passenger in a train stopped at a station catching sight of a friend in another train that has pulled up alongside; proximity but not overdone proximity.

'What I'm getting at is, we are asked by the present, very current principal, Sir Bert Greg-Peterson, to decide on how the university should honour two past principals, two sequen-tial past principals who had limited respect for each other,' Upp said. 'Thus begins the process I've referred to. It might appear at first to be a straightforward administrative task. "Pray give me feedback on what we should do with these putative two lumps of stone or brass." Naturally, however, as Greg-Peterson initiates this process he is bound to throw his mind forward into the unknown future, when the present principal, viz, Sir Bert, has himself become a past principal and therefore due a statue in his turn. "The king is dead or retired or gone to a bigger job. Long live the king, as monument." Sir Bert will be interested in this process, as a guide to a similar process in the future, of which he will be the subject; while at the same time taking part himself, now, not as subject but as originator in the present, 2014 process. Some future Sedge principal will request a special working party, comparable with ours in 2014, to discuss the type of statue needed for Greg-Peterson and the most suitable site for it, if it is to be a single permanent site; or a duality of sites, if a rotation is favoured, taking in what will by then be the strongly estab-lished single university with paired campuses, which at present might still be lingeringly, wrongly, but forgivably thought of as Charter Mill and Sedge, or Sedge and Charter Mill.

'Admittedly, certain differences between those future

proceedings and our own are going to exist. I'll name one: the kind of debate we had over single or double plinth occupancy will not be appropriate then, since the commemorative statue and its mono-plinth would be for one past principal only – Sir Bert – not, as in the 2014 case, Chote and Tane or Tane and Chote, each with formidable *prima facie* entitlement, each requiring and deserving fair play.

'That future planning group would have to take into account that there were already two ex-principal statues on university sites, or *a* university site if, eventually, we decide on a binary plinth for two statues, one at each end of it, Chote and Tane, or, to phrase it differently, Tane and Chote. The present principal will be thinking as he considers our findings on the Tane, Chote, or Chote, Tane statues, how, in that on-coming future, he would like his own statue sited in relation to the already placed – locationed, if you will – statues of Tane and Chote or Chote and Tane.

'Several questions would need consideration, the central one being, should the Sir Bert statue be close to or distant from the by then existing Chote/Tane, Tane/Chote statues? If these two are single plinthed and therefore very near each other, more or less plinth-integrated, might the Sir Bert statue seem somehow set-apart if it were deposited close to the pair but not, of course, as close as the two single-plinthed figures would be to each other? Might the Sir Bert image seem excluded, even shunned, by the two in this case? Or, to reverse it, would the Sir Bert statue appear snooty and stand-offish, aloof, as if proclaiming that the other two were elements of an exceptionally messy Sedge, Charter Mill, or Charter Mill, Sedge past, redeemed by the power and brilliance of the masterly, remote, true leader, Sir Bertram?

'If, on the other hand, the 2014 decision is to go for single statues of Chote and Tane or Tane and Chote, should the Greg-Peterson statue be put adjacent to one of them, and, if so, which one would it be? More rotation? Or are further permutations envisaged? Finally, might it be best to unfix Chote and Tane, or Tane and Chote, from their shared plinth and devise a larger plinth able to provide room not just for Tane and Chote, or Chote and Tane, but Sir Bert, also. Clearly this would require skilled stonemasonry, or brassmasonry, so that the two's shoes and feet should not be fractured during the severance, but it *could* be feasible. However, a threesome on one plinth would give rise to additional, obvious contentiousness. Two on one plinth did not suggest any kind of precedence. One end of a plinth represents no superiority or inferiority to the other end. Each statue would be at the end it was, right or left, left or right, simply because it was – no overtones. But triple-plinthed statues must plainly imply a central figure. Might centrality suggest dominance, distinction, as if the other two, one on each side, were aides only or minders? Which statue would occupy this middle position?

'If order of plinth alignment were decided by length of existence and chronology, then perhaps Chote would come first, on the left, because of Sedge's age, then Tane, head of the younger institution, then Sir Bert, as principal of a very new combined entity. This would, accordingly, put Tane in the mid position. There might not be general agreement about that. Tane could be regarded by some as jumped-up. They might argue that the new university under Sir Bert subsumes both previous universities and, therefore, his statue should dominate, that is, should be at the plinth's core and central. We have to keep in mind that Sir Bert *is* Sir Bert – he has a knighthood, which neither of his predecessors achieved. Perhaps a central spot on a tripartite plinth would be his proper due.

'This is what I mean when I say that the process we engage in now, here, 2014, is more than itself in that our present principal will be virtually bound to use our process as a start-up for thoughts of an imaginary but comparable statue planning committee trying to decide the most suitable style and emplacement for his – Sir Bert's – post-retirement statue, possibly on a unitary plinth share basis, possibly otherwise.'

'But could it not be, Gordon, that the statue creating mode for ex-principals will no longer apply when our present principal, Sir Bert, might be dead or of an age and/or situation that would put him into the potentially appropriate category for the tribute of a statue?' Wayne Ollam (Philosophy) said. 'I feel there is already something of a distaste for the manufacture of statues to mark supposed achievements of a selected figure. Perhaps there's something crazy about representing in stone or brass a person whose life has been characterized by dynamic activity. We have, after all, the phrase "stone dead", meaning very dead. Maybe there is much of that about statues.

'Then again, isn't a statue discriminatory? Of its nature it discounts credit for all those non-statued folk who might have provided essential help for the one acknowledged star. We've heard a while ago about the statue of Aneurin Bevan in the commercial centre of Cardiff, the Welsh politician who helped create the National Health Service. But, obviously, doctors, nurses, consultants, administrators, other politicians were involved in that. Do any of them get statues in a shopping mall? No. And by the time Sir Bert qualifies public disenchantment with statues might have become even stronger. The principal we are visualising – i.e., not Sir Bert but the one who comes after Sir Bert, and is therefore faced by the Sir Bert statue problem – this new principal might be of a socio-political academic background and averse to the creation, indeed the proliferation, of statues on the kind of democratic grounds I have just referred to: elitism.'

'Widmerpool questions whether a statue is the right way to commemorate a great man,' Elvira Barton (Classics) said.

'Who?' Bill Davey (French) replied.

'Kenneth Widmerpool,' Jed Laver (Industrial Relations) said. 'He's already been mentioned – a comical, plonking, rather dangerous character in Anthony Powell's twelve-volume novel *A Dance To The Music Of Time*.'

'Yes, in *A Buyer's Market* – second book of the sequence – people at a dinner party are discussing what would be the right sort of statue to honour Earl Haig,' Angela Drape (Environmental Engineering) said.

'A dinner at the Walpole-Wilson's in Eaton Square, London, I think,' Claud Nelmes (Physics) said. '*Circa* 1928.'

'Haig led the British Expeditionary Force in the Great War. Butcher Haig as he was sometimes known, because of the millions of soldiers killed,' Elvira said. 'Powell is mocking this kind of lumbering, slightly zany conversation – should Haig be shown on a horse, or in a car or at a desk? Someone suggests a *papier mâché* model of a horse to ensure accuracy. Widmerpool says statues could cause traffic problems.'

'But the principals' statues will be on university ground, surely,' Theo said. 'Traffic wouldn't be affected.'

'We are concerned with the principles,' Ollam said.

'Yes, I know it's about the principals – Principal Bert and the other two,' Theo said.

'The principles,' Ollam said. 'The general question of whether statues are the kind of thing wanted these days to indicate worth.'

'There's a town called Widmerpool, in Cheshire, I believe,' Davey said. 'Perhaps this Widmerpool gent thought he, personally, wouldn't need a statue because he had a town named after him. Therefore statues should be phased out.'

'I think it was the other way about,' Jed said.

'Which other way?' Davey asked.

'Powell named the character after the town,' Jed replied. 'The town pre-existed the fictional person. Philip Larkin, the poet, slammed Powell for pinching a name like that.'

'Does Larkin have a statue?' Davey asked.

'He was very tall, wasn't he, maybe as tall as Victor Tane?' Theo said.

'Lucy argued a while back that one or two of our presumptions about the statues might be open to question – the plinth matter, for instance,' Wayne Ollam replied. 'But I want to ask whether our absolutely basic assumption – that there should be statues at all – might have been too hastily arrived at. Should we really be niggling over structural and positional details? Isn't there a case for recommending that there should be no statues at all, neither the Chote, nor the Tane, nor the Tane nor the Chote, let alone the fantasized, forecasted Sir Bert?'

Mart Moss said, 'But we've been asked by the principal – in fact, more or less instructed by the principal, Sir Bert – to come up with a plan for installing the statues, Wayne. This would appear to endorse the provision of statues, wouldn't it?'

'Ostensibly, yes,' Wayne replied. 'I would like to ask, though, whether in his thinking about the statues of his predecessors and therefore also speculating mentally about his own, in due course, statue, he will sense that perhaps in the 21st century – and possibly much further on in the 21st century entailing continuous, deep, rapid social change – he might sense that statues will have become *infra dig* and super-naff. He might decide he will not need a statue, that, in fact, a statue would be otiose and vain. And this could cause him to think that even now, at this earlier 21st-century date, statues have become redundant, corny, gross, as well as incapable of showing the actual energy he brought to his career. He'd possibly come to regard statues as objects to stick piss-pots on the stone heads of or to daub with painted ribaldries, such as "Show us your arse."

'He finds himself, however, in the grip of snobbish tradition rather than free to follow his private conclusions, and, accordingly, he commissions us to devise a practicable scheme for the Chote, Tane or Tane, Chote memorials. Does it strike nobody else here that he might wish to be liberated from all those trite pressures and expectations? Might it not be an act of mercy to go to him and say, "Sir Bert, we find after several *causeries* carried out in the best, balanced, higher-education style that we are of a concerted mind which says statues are unholy shit and the Tane, Chote or Chote, Tane project should be finally and irretrievably flushed away."

'There is, of course, one outstanding reason why memorials are regarded with scepticism now, though perhaps we would not put this to Sir Bert. It has an element of controversy about it. I'm sure some of you would understand what I mean.'

'The Jimmy Savile headstone,' Theo said, 'with that appalling inscription, "It was good while it lasted."'

'Exactly,' Wayne replied.

'"Philanthropist", another of the inscriptions,' Theo said.

'The *Sir* Jimmy, O.B.E. headstone,' Wayne said. 'This memorial in a Scarborough cemetery was four feet high and six feet wide. It reeked of praise for a man whose life had seemed devoted to good causes, especially good causes aimed at helping children. In fact he was a rampant, scheming paedophile and used his secret closeness to some children for sex. He had a television spot called *Jim'll Fix It*. This was supposedly concerned with granting selected children something they wished for, dreamed of. It's actual purpose, though, was to fix things for himself sexually. Likewise, he presented a music programme called *Top of the Pops*, which gave him access to young fans of the show.

'When the truth about him emerged after his death the black granite headstone came to be seen as a disgusting, lying monstrosity and it was demolished and sent as landfill by his family. I'm not saying that the statues of Victor Tane and/or Lawford Chote, or Lawford Chote and/or Victor Tane would get destroyed, but I *am* saying that people looking at memorials these days and, no doubt, in future days, no matter what form they take, wonder whether the tribute is deserved or a cover-up for the remembered one's real life.'

Moss said, 'This will certainly give us something to think over before our next scheduled *causerie*, Wayne. Thank you.'

NINETEEN

1987

CENTENARY CONCERT AT d'BRINDLE HALL
By O.T.O. Jurbb, Music Correspondent

Last night's musical event at the city's brand new d'Brindle Hall marked the opening of three weeks' celebration in honour of Sedge University's centenary year. Some will see a chilling comparison between this ambitious, glittering occasion and the so-said re-arranging of deck chairs on the *Titanic* as she sank. Others might recall Thomas Hardy's poem, *The Convergence of the Twain,* which described the luxurious fitting out of the liner during construction, while the iceberg that would slash the vessel open was also under construction, but meteorological construction, growing bigger and more dangerous at the Pole, ready to 'converge'. A similar sort of grim convergence might have been in the air yesterday evening at the d'Brindle: high, splendid ambition in deadly collision with Sedge's massive debts and near bankruptcy. As E.M. Forster nearly said, 'Only connect the prose of this review and the poverty.'

For the Sedge concert to take place in the d'Brindle Hall could be seen as painfully ironic. The d'Brindle is a magnificent, very recent addition to the Sedge campus and is named after the distinguished British composer and conductor, Harvey d'Brindle, a former student and subsequently professor of music at Sedge, who died a few years ago. His widow, Martha Maud d'Brindle was present last night. She heard one of her husband's most famous works, the gigue, *Cumulus Resurgent*, played with reasonable vim and competence by a section of the orchestra.

The unpaid builder's account for d'Brindle Hall is one of the university's major debts. To a cruel degree it typifies the kind of cash difficulty afflicting Sedge. The fine new, acoustically perfect venue, is very much the brainchild and darling of Dr Lawford Chote, Sedge's principal. He, unquestionably, provided the original impetus for creation of the d'Brindle and has diligently guided and nursed the project through the not-always-positive and/or helpful intricacies of governmental and/or academic bureaucracy. The d'Brindle is, in some ways, a tribute to Dr Chote as much as it is to Harvey d'Brindle.

But this tribute to the principal comes with a bill. And it is a millions sterling bill. The number of millions has not been disclosed. Guesses range from £4 million to £12 million. At any rate, formidable. Good acoustics don't come cheap. Sedge has so far failed to pay. Sedge *can't* pay. Knowledgeable folk in the audience last night might have been glancing back over their shoulders in case the duns and bum-bailiffs arrived with something other than gigues in their minds. The d'Brindle is, perhaps, the most flagrant instance of what can be seen as Dr Chote's heady, audacious, thrilling but devilishly pricey, expansionism. There are others on campus, including an impressive new curved staircase, carpeted in azure blue, leading to the

grandly refurbished staff dining room and bar, a stairway
to the stars, or to the cliff's edge.

Dr Chote is himself an accomplished amateur musician,
specialising in percussion and particularly the cymbals. At
the concert he gave a short, cameo performance of a piece
from Wagner's *Tannhauser.* As he clashed those two
shining brass discs together at pretty well exactly the right
dramatic moments one could see the challenging sound as
defiance, a sort of Bronx cheer, aimed at those who regard
his principalship as disastrous, and want him kicked out
while there might still be time to save Sedge under a new
chief and a more sane regime.

Dr Chote is not a big man and has a sensitive, pale,
aquiline, nunnish sort of face, but the force he could get
into smashing those two cymbals together seemed ferocious. Your critic half expected him to stick his tongue
out at any enemies in the hall between each ultra-
decibelled bang. His features showed no feelings, though.
He remained virtually deadpan except for a scarcely
perceptible, flickering hint that he kept an orderly, vindictive pack of hatreds kennelled within him and might turn
it loose at any time he'd regard as appropriate and/or
destructive.

Reading this review in the local daily, Martin Moss wondered
whether O.T.O. Jurbb was an alias for Alan Norton-Hord, editor
of the paper, who'd seemed so investigative and clued-up about
the Sedge predicament in the grandly refurbished bar and staff
dining room, immediately after Mart's inaugural spiel about
rural rogering as a newly promoted prof. Editors sometimes
took pen names so that personal views should not be regarded
as the views of the paper. There were *people* called Jurbb? But
in a multi-cultural country there might be.

Mart couldn't remember ever having seen this by-line in the
paper before. He'd noticed Norton-Hord at the concert last night,
but he might have been attending as a civic dignitary, not as
critic and reporter. Was Norton-Hord the kind who would
flourish his familiarity with Thomas Hardy and Morgan Forster?
As an ex-Sedge student, would he write so bluntly about the

university being near-fatally hard-up? Would he spray the faint
praise around: the performance of *Cumulus Resurgent* done
with 'reasonable' vim and competence; the timing of Lawford
Chote's interventions with the cymbals at 'pretty well exactly
the right dramatic moments' in the *Tannhauser* clip? Would
O.T.O. Jurbb?

Mart Moss didn't go much on classical music so he couldn't
judge whether the performance of *Cumulus Resurgent* was only
just up to scratch; nor whether Lawford Chote had the timing
of his cymbal flurries right. Watching Chote with the instru-
ments had reminded Mart of some B.B.C. television archive
material re-broadcast lately in a programme on changing
comedy styles. A small, baby-faced, bald performer called
Charlie Drake had done some cymbal bashing with an orchestra
and after each echoing, metallic boom looked totally dazed,
as if the din had morphed into solid form and clobbered his
head. Jurbb, in his column, had called Chote's appearance at
those aftermath moments 'deadpan'. Martin thought 'concussed'
more to the point. But he would agree with Jurbb's suggestion
that the clangour caused by Lawford carried a message of
defiance, contempt, war, for those who wanted his humiliation
and defeat. There might be a further show of defiance when
the centenary celebrations culminated in the Plain Parlour
banquet at Standfast Fort.

Cymbals in Lawford's hands might also have been useful in
keeping Rowena awake. She had a front row seat. Mart was
some way behind and could not see her face, but she hadn't
slumped and seemed to do a little shoulder dance during a movement from one of the Mozart symphonies. Moss reckoned music
started to fall away after the seventeenth century, and definitely
by the time Mozart started. This didn't mean Mart would go
along with Jim Dixon's description of Wolfgang Amadeus in
Lucky Jim as 'filthy Mozart'. What people should remember
about Mozart was that he had to write much of his stuff for
paying patrons who might be laid up at home with gout and/or
a double dose of pox. They wouldn't object that a composition
was full of phoney joyous, scampering, bubbly riffs. To be
reminded of joy, and the ability to scamper, and/or something
bubbly in any form would be a plus for them. But Mart preferred,

say, Henry Purcell's neat, unshowy, purposeful songs and anthems about a hundred years earlier, and British with it.

Moss read some more of Jurbb.

> Although several of the items on the centenary concert menu were executed with no more than workmanlike efficiency, we have to be grateful that the musicians turned up and played at all when, most probably, they had no assurance there would be a cashable cheque to follow. Despite all the rumours – and more than rumours – about impending disaster, the combined names of Sedge and Lawford Chote have been enough to make a function like last night's possible and to a not inconsiderable sense successful. Although Sedge and Lawford Chote are perilously short of cash, they still have charisma.

Yes, Mart could say 'Agreed' to this.

TWENTY

1987

R
owena and Lawford Chote also read the O.T.O. Jurbb review next morning. It gave them a few good laughs. They were in bed. They had a pre-breakfast daybreak routine. Soon after the newspapers had been delivered, she or he – an alternating duty – would go downstairs to pick them up, then return, snuggle under the duvet again and for half an hour or so read bits to each other and perhaps view some of the more striking photographs together. If there were exciting pictures of, say, the return of otters to a stretch of river somewhere, or a seascape, or an arboretum, or a starlings' flight-swarm, they might take a break from the press for a while and make leisurely love, so as to link up, as it were, with nature. Breakfast could be delayed for a while. She thought more of nature than Lawford did, but he wasn't actually anti and would go along with Rowena.

It would have been wise before starting sex if they'd folded the newspapers and put them on the floor or a bedside table. But both felt this would seem too calculated and unimpassioned, as though they had to abide by an etiquette book *diktat:* 'Always clear away surplus items before coitus.' If they wanted a sort of inspired link with thousands of soaring, swooping starlings they couldn't take time out to make some press sheets dailies tidy. As a result pages could get badly crumpled and even torn because of the threshing about. If they were smoothable-out afterwards Rowena or Lawford would smooth them out. Torn pages might be repairable with transparent sticky tape. They kept some of that in the bedside table drawer along with scissors and a stiff-backed copy of the proper, King James version of the Bible. Now and then they'd enjoy a joint reading of a Psalm, one doing the first, strong line of a verse, the other coming in with the backup. A favourite at present for Lawford, as could be expected, was: 'Plead my cause, oh Lord, with them that strive with me: fight against them that fight against me.'

The concert review didn't set them off hormonally but did produce major non-sexual chuckles. 'Yes, Ro, I think it does what we wanted,' Lawford said, 'that sort of back-handed praise: nothing too lavish and sloppy. So, only *reasonable* vim and competence given to *Cumulus Resurgent.* And then, my *pretty well* timed cymbal wallops.'

'The *Titanic* references work OK, I think, don't you?' she replied. 'They'll get through to people's feelings. Decent, sensitive folk will say we had that terrible tragedy all those years ago, so why haven't we learned from it?'

Lawford giggled. 'I liked "acoustics don't come cheap". Slangy but terse-effective. And then those in the audience who couldn't concentrate on the music because they were afraid the bums were about to arrive and strip the place! A hoot.'

They both had guffaws at this idea, and, possibly, at an imagined glimpse of Lawford sticking his tongue out and/or giving a raspberry to his opponents between clashes on the pretty well-timed cymbal detonations. Sitting up in bed they did a duet of fart noises with their lips.

'How's my charisma looking today, Ro?' he said.

She put her head under the duvet. 'Seems fine to me,' she replied.

Lawford went through the review again. 'The "stairway to the stars" that turns into a lemming-drop. Great, Ro! And the internal hate kennels! "Cry Havoc! and let slip the dogs of war." Wonderful!'

'It wasn't easy, you know, Lawf.'

'I can see that.'

'I didn't want it to sound abject and self-pitying yet to be, in fact, an appeal for understanding and sympathy.'

'You hit that. It will help us.'

'And not biased – not biased in favour of you and Sedge. I had to promise Alan Norton-Hord that, before he'd let me do it. He wants to help Sedge – past chairman of the students' union and so on. But he's editor now of a respectable provincial paper and has to seem to be fair and impartial.'

'Maybe.'

'I had to phrase things here and there to sound blunt and dogmatic – "Sedge has so far failed to pay. Sedge *can't* pay." But my review's overall objective was to make people – especially government people – yes, the objective was to make them ask whether it was sane to let Sedge go under like the *Titanic* because the university's finances couldn't keep up with the principal's noble, life-enhancing, splendiferous, aims.'

'The "O.T.O.", Ro? What were Mr or Mrs or Miss or Ms's Jurbb's first names?'

'"Only This Once". The gender and family ranking are immaterial.'

TWENTY-ONE

2014

A couple of weeks later they had a vote on Wayne Ollam's proposal to recommend a no-statue, no-statues policy, and he was the only one in favour He took the thrashing without any obvious sign of disbelief or rage. He was a philosopher and knew about stoicism and the dominance of naffdom and knee-jerk in others. Wryly, almost graciously, he said, 'So sodding be it.'

But some of the committee seemed sorry for him, embarrassed for him. Ollam had a round, jolly-looking, schoolboyish, snub-nosed face under blondish curls, and Mart could see that some committee members felt it brutal having to humiliate him. As a sort of compensation several people became more bolshy-aggressive than usual, perhaps to prove they were no pushovers; not slavishly choosing to carry on with the project because they thought the principal wanted it. The sniping began after Theo Bastrolle had floated a new idea.

He said, 'Something at first sight extraneous, but actually quite to the point, I think, has startled me. Startled and baffled me. I wondered if other members had felt the same.'

'The same as what?' Angela Drape (Environmental Engineering) said in her curt, barrack-square bellow.

'It's very simply put,' Theo replied.

'Put it,' Angela said.

'Here goes then. I suddenly noticed that we have no member of the music department among our number,' Theo said. 'Am I the only one who has spotted this grave lack? I doubt it.'

'Grave?' Lucy Lane (History) said.

Theo said, 'Oh, I recognize that someone might reply, "So what, there are several departments unrepresented here. No Chemistry. No Geography. No Maths. Omissions are inevitable or the meetings would become unwieldy." Fair enough. But I regard Music as very much a special case.'

'In what respect, Theo?' Jed Laver (Industrial Relations) asked. 'I don't see it. What is so precious and unusual about Music?'

'A building,' Theo replied.

'Yes, yes, there's a building, d'Brindle Hall,' Jed said. 'Nobody can deny that. Yet I still ask, why should we give particular attention to Music, d'Brindle or no?'

'It's not "or no," though, is it, Jed? It is very much an emphatic "Yes".' Theo said.

'Why "emphatic"?' Bill Davey (French) said.

'I lived through that period here, so think I might see what Theo means,' Martin Moss said.

'Oh?' Lucy Lane replied.

'Thank you, Chair,' Theo said.

'Thank him for what?' Davey said.

'To do with d'Brindle,' Mart said.

'What about it?' Jed replied.

'We have to think of our purpose here. Our *raison d'être* as a committee,' Theo said.

Gordon Upp (Linguistics) said, 'Oh, *d'être* and d'Brindle! What *is* this?'

'Remember that old song, "It's delightful, it's delicious, it's d'lovely"?' Elvira (Classics) asked. 'Cole Porter?'

'What it is, Gordon, and what we are,' Theo stated, 'is a committee established to discuss and eventually recommend the most suitable – in our view – the most suitable siting for, and nature of, a statue or, more likely, statues, as a tribute to two distinguished past principals. We act at the behest of our present distinguished principal who may or may not be thinking of how his own period of office might be commemorated when his time at Sedge is done one way or the other.'

Mart said, 'Theo, like the majority here, has moved away from the option that there should be no statue, Gordon. He has returned to the basic requirement of our committee – to choose a site or sites. And, since the d'Brindle is a building with some lawn in front – is, in fact, potentially a statue site – he is wondering why this has not come previously into our reckoning.'

'Thank you, Chair,' Theo said.

'Oh, is this a put-up job?' Claud Nelmes (Physics) said.

'Is what a put-up job?' Mart replied.

'You two.' Claud made his voice slimy, grovelling. '"Thank you, Chair." Have you agreed *sub rosa* beforehand that you'd back each other up – tout the Music department's case jointly?'

'There's no backing up, Claud. I summarized what I took to be Theo's standpoint,' Martin said.

'Summarized it favourably,' Jed replied. 'Where's the chair's impartiality, Chair? Why can't Theo speak for himself? You've pre-worked out a scenario between you, yes? You've decided that from now on all major decisions should be made by the chair, because that will seem unbiased and, authoritative?'

'I've been looking at the d'Brindle papers in the Sedge archive,' Theo replied.

'To what purpose?' Angela said.

'We've heard from various sections of both archives, Charter's and Sedge's, or Sedge's and Tane's, but I don't think anyone has looked at the d'Brindle file,' Theo said. 'The Sedge papers show very clearly that Lawford Chote was the main force in getting the d'Brindle built,' Theo said.

'I can endorse that,' Mart said. 'Many of us at Sedge then knew it.'

'Ah!' Lucy said. 'Deduction: he should have his statue placed in front of the d'Brindle. That your argument, Theo?' Her thin face seemed to grow even sharper when she reached this question.

'A sort of Euterpe figure,' Elvira said.

'A what?' Angela said.

'The muse of music,' Jed said. 'My parents were going to call me that if I'd been a girl. But I wanted to go for industrial relations, anyway.'

'Chote himself was an amateur musician, apparently,' Theo said.

'Playing what?' Lucy said.

'Cymbals,' Theo said.

'Do we recommend a statue of Chote banging a couple of them together in front of his chest?' Davey asked.

'There's a review of a centenary concert in the file,' Theo replied. 'Chote actually took part. A piece from *Tannhauser* required cymbals. The review's slightly snooty – implies Lawford didn't quite get the timing right during the performance.'

'Cymbals sticking in a shattering sound at the wrong spot could fuck up the whole item,' Angela said.

'The New Testament has a "tinkling" cymbal,' Nelmes said.

'*Tannhauser* would want something stronger than a tinkle,' Davey said.

'Who wrote the notice?' Jed asked.

'An O.T.O Jurbb,' Theo said.

'Otto, do you mean?' Davey said. 'Like Klemperer and Bismark.'

'No, O.T.O.,' Theo said. 'He or she makes a meal of the contrast between the glittering social occasion and Sedge's desperate lack of funds. There are comparisons with the *Titanic*.'

'The *Titanic*? That's cruel, heartless,' Claud Nelmes said. 'The reviewer would know the *Titanic* went down. He or she couldn't have the same certainty at the time of the concert that Sedge was about to sink. At least, Sedge as it had existed for a hundred years up till then.'

'This was supposed to be a critique of some music, wasn't it, not an attempt at clairvoyance,' Elvira said.

'What you said, Claud – "cruel", "heartless" – is possibly correct but it was also a warning. I think, and a disguised cry for help,' Theo replied.

'A very subtle piece of journalism,' Bill Davey said.

'I'll have it copied and circulated,' Theo replied. 'Tucked in with the newspaper review I found two reports by accountants showing a debt on the d'Brindle building and fitments of between £9 and £10 million,' Theo said. 'Incidentally, other considerable unpaid bills were for new student accommodation blocks as part of Chote's expansion programme. But, regardless of these enormous shortfalls, what comes over in the concert review, and what the contemporary reader would sense, is the fine, positive, determined, effort through this concert to take forward Sedge's reputation as a top-class creative, cultural university. One feels these debts were . . . would it be foolishly exaggerated to say *noble* debts? I get the feeling that Lawford had contempt for the strictures of finance.'

'"Tax not the royal saint with vain expense",' Lucy replied.

'Who said that?' Angela asked.

'Wordsworth, a sonnet, about King's college chapel, Cambridge, founded by Henry VI,' Lucy said. '"High-heaven rejects the lore/ Of nicely calculated less or more".'

'Whitehall didn't though,' Angela snarled.

'The review ends with a powerful accolade to Chote's and Sedge's charisma,' Theo said.

'How do we get the sculptor to give us charisma in stone or

brass?' Upp asked. 'We've already fretted over how to portray ambiguity.'

'Are we talking now about a Chote statue either with or without cymbals installed at the d'Brindle?' Nelmes asked.

'Victor Tane would have nothing to balance,' Jed said.

'Balance how, what?' Theo asked.

'Nothing equivalent to the cymbals held by Chote, if they were,' Jed said. 'Tane might appear deprived, comparatively untalented as to cymbals and possibly music generally.'

'If we go for two statues on the one plinth, Chote and Tane will look not so much like muses as a couple of duetists because of the d'Brindle Hall, Music department background,' Upp said.

'Ah, such as the old Bing Crosby-Bob Hope record?' Elvira said. She would often go out of her way to show she could handle more than the Classics and other heavy stuff, such as the Book of Amos. Mart learned today that Cole Porter and Bing and Bob were also on call when it suited, or, as now, when it didn't.

Elvira crooned effortlessly, in two different voices, one tenor, one alto, beating time with her small hands, her pale blue eyes alight with joy as she fondled the irrelevant melody: 'We're off on the road to Morocco, de-dum-de-dum, I'll lay you eight to four we'll meet Dorothy Lamour, de-dum-de-dum, Like Webster's dictionary we're Morocco bound.'

'Tane, of course, has no real connection with the d'Brindle,' Lucy said.

'Tane helped turn its finances around,' Angela replied. 'And so the d'Brindle is still there, still housing good concerts.'

'I went online to the Newspaper Archive in London and Googled for an O.T.O. Jurbb around in the 1980s. Nothing,' Theo said. 'I tried anagrams in case this was a pen name only: Rob Jobut, Jo Burbot, but blank.'

'No, I'd never read anything previously by him or her at the time,' Mart said.

'Rob Jobut – there's a name to conjure with,' Davey said.

'And what do you get when you conjure?' Theo asked.

'O.T.O. Jurbb,' Davey replied.

TWENTY-TWO

1987

Victor Tane read the review of last night's Sedge centenary concert a couple of times at breakfast and then passed it to his wife, Ursula. She was a lawyer, trained to see behind what people said and wrote. She had a lively, squarish face very ready to go into a grin but ready, also, to turn combative if antagonized by something or somebody. She was middle-height, neat-breasted, and slim. She'd gone auburn lately, a good, restrained but rich shade, worn as a fringe across her forehead and gathered into a clasped bunch at the back. 'O.T.O?' she muttered. 'Is that supposed to be Otto, like Klemperer and Bismark?'

'Not sure. I've never heard of a writer called O.T.O Jurbb, nor Otto Jurbb.'

'Nor me. Weird surname, too. Might the two bits – O.T.O. and Jurbb – be an anagram of the writer's real moniker?'

'I've considered that.'

'Jo Burbot?' Ursula said.

'Rob Jobut?' Tane replied. 'Names to conjure with.'

'What do you get when you conjure, Vic?'

'O.T.O. Jurbb.'

Ursula forked in scrambled egg while she read. She was thirty-five, Tane's third wife. He was her second husband. Tane had an adult son, a TV director, by his first wife. 'Clever,' Ursula said. She swallowed carefully, thoroughly, then grinned one of her big, jolly grins, no egg traces on her teeth or lips; Ursula was not the sort to allow that kind of facial unkempt-ness. Tane thought her grin would be part in admiration of the cleverness, whatever it was, and part in admiration of her own cleverness in seeing through the cleverness, whatever it was. Ursula had a flair for making him feel stupid. He'd wondered sometimes whether she'd done the same to her previous husband, which might have helped towards the divorce. He had been an MP. The job itself could have made him feel stupid and he wouldn't want that at home as well. Anyway, if Tane wished to ponder the reasons for a divorce he realized he should consider his own two; and he didn't fancy this.

'Clever?' he replied.

'The *Titanic* pushed up to the front like that. Necessary first sentence to tell us where we're at, then straight into catastrophe.'

'Tactical?'

'The sea-worm,' Ursula replied.

'Which?'

'The one in the *Convergence* poem. We did it at school. The *Titanic* is on the seabed and over its luxury bits and pieces "The sea-worm crawls – grotesque, slimed, dumb, indifferent."'

'Dumb? Don't sea-worms talk to one another?'

'Sets a tone from the outset.'

'What tone?'

'Hardy's a nasty piece of work, isn't he?' she replied.

'Is he?'

'Getting a smirk out of the disaster. This was a fine ship. Brave funnels. OK, it had luxurious, lavishly, ostentatiously costly fittings and good deckchairs, but so what? Is it an offence to do things in style? Yes, he gets a smirk and/or a snigger at the thought of all this flagrant privilege going to the bottom because of a ripening berg. That title.'

'*Convergence*? Bad?'

'It's loaded with septic irony, Vic. Normally, it would be a neutral, map-reading term. Here it means two mighty big items both trying to get on the same spot at the same time. Procrastinated doom: for ages, the berg has been preparing itself for this jostle by making sure the deadly seven eighths of itself below the surface is all present and malicious. In other words, Vic, those *Titanic* references seem to mock Sedge but actually indict others – Whitehall, the Ministry – for threatening to bring destruction to it. And then the Forster quote tacked on: the prose of the review wants to highlight Sedge's poverty and induce those able to put all that right, to put it all right – Whitehall, the Ministry. I wouldn't be surprised if someone close to Chote wrote this, with his connivance.'

'I gather he's got a new acolyte over there. We have a picture of them in a Volvo. Him perhaps? If he's on the Humanities staff he might have the literary allusions ready – Hardy, E.M. Forster.'

'Maybe. Or possibly Rowena. She would have to seem detached, even harsh, but the real intent is something different. She'd use unfriendly phrases like "devilishly pricey expansionism" and "vindictive pack of hatreds" as a kind of camouflage to conceal her authorship.'

'Rowena?'

'She's smart enough and had an education. She gets in a slab of praise for Lawford Chote – creating the d'Brindle, his "brainchild and darling", but then has to spout a virtual retraction so as to seem objective – the "millions sterling bill" which "Sedge *can't* pay". Doesn't someone who could conceive the d'Brindle deserve a handout? That's the message. And then that brilliant contrast.'

'Which, Ursula?'

'Between Harvey d'Brindle and Lawford Chote, of course.'

'How does that work?'

'We have Harvey d'Brindle, more or less a genius, known worldwide, especially for his gigues e.g., *Cumulus Resurgent*; as against Chote doing his approximate best with the cymbals but not at all a gifted star like d'Brindle. Chote makes his wellmeant but faulty contribution to *Tannhauser*, an opera about a singing competition, and one he'd ruin with his mistimed cymbals. interventions. But the review is saying that as an undergraduate and graduate even the natural prodigy, H. d'Brindle, needed opportunities to develop those in-born qualities, such opportunities being provided by somewhere like Sedge, headed by one of Chote's predecessors as principal. This is a debt d'Brindle acknowledged by joining Sedge's staff and making some of his talent available to new generations of students.

'The review's point, surely, Vic, is that even a wonderful composer and performer like d'Brindle, can do with the guidance and backing of a Sedge-type apprenticeship. To let the university dwindle and perhaps die because of a temporary shortage of boodle is, O.T.O. Jurbb believes, an example of idiotic, short-sighted vandalism. He/she is telling the Education Minister, "Cough up, you fucking philistines." Those benighted Whitehall people would send in duns and bums because – to go poetic – Lawford Chote has no regard for sums. But not even those low-grade, disgusting terms can do irreparable harm to Sedge and Chote because their "charisma" still works, and will go on working for as long as the miserable, workaday banalities of special funding are taken care of. The fact that the musicians agreed to play even though they might not get paid showed the pulling power exercised by Sedge and Chote.'

Ursula went off to appear in a court case. Tane could linger for another half hour. He washed up and took a cup of coffee to his study. He felt like writing to his mother. 'Ursula sees a real crisis for the other university here at Sedge, Ma. She sort of deconstructed a review in the local paper and found it to be a rather sneaky, roundabout demand for more money from central government to keep Sedge afloat, saving it from foundering like the *Titanic*. I don't believe the money will arrive. This has obvious implications for Charter Mill and myself. Part of me feels quite sorry for the principal over there, Lawford Chote.'

If his mother had still been alive and received this he thought she would probably reply something like: 'Which part of you feels quite sorry, you gaunt and gangling twerp? Remember, I'm the one who gave you all your parts and none of them should show weakness. Stop patronising. Be a winner. Come out from between your goalposts, surge through the astonished opposition and score the clinching goal that ensures promotion.'

TWENTY-THREE

2014

Her voice gentle and considerate, Elvira Barton (Classics) said, 'Wayne recently asked us to look at, and pronounce upon, the very existence of the statues theme and decide whether we should recommend abandonment of the project, which would put us out of existence also! We gave an answer, and, what I believe it's fair to term, an unambiguous one, an answer which Wayne has honourably accepted. I'm sure we would have expected nothing other from him.'

'Here, here,' Angela Drape (Environmental Engineering) said.

'*Absolument*,' Bill Davey (French) said.

Seated between Gordon Upp (Linguistics) and Lucy Lane (History) Wayne Ollam (Philosophy) gave a small nod-bow in acknowledgement and some curls fell forward on to his brow, like rounds from a disturbed sliced loaf. Unhurriedly, he pushed them back with the spread fingers of his ringless right hand. The whole exchange had a simple, but emphatic dignity. To Mart, those fingers looked for the moment like fingers which knew they were among top-grade stuff, even if the curls belonged to someone crash-ball annihilated in a vote not long ago.

'And, despite the way our moot went then, I feel I have learned something from Wayne's boldness in scrutinising the very fundamentals of our duties,' Elvira said. 'He humbly included himself in his suggestion that we might have been hasty and careless in not questioning why the statues committee had come into being. Perhaps our vote negated that criticism. But it taught me that this is the kind of head-on confrontation we should practise with all aspects of our musing and mulling. For instance, and this brings me to my point, the matter of equality. Now, equality is a very fine thing. None of us would deny that, I'm sure.' She stopped. Mart thought some talented pre-planning, even rehearsal, had gone into this.

'Well . . . no . . . I'm *not* sure!' she said, the 'not' categorical, aggressive.

Martin recognized one of the standard tricks by lecturers to stop students dozing off: the deliberate error, followed by a wake-up-at-the-back-there correction.

'This uncertainty is why I'm badgering you with my spiel now,' she said. 'It is the kind of re-think that Wayne's courageous initiative has caused me. Slavishly – and a little farcically at times – we have striven to avoid giving either of the universities and either of the principals any sort of precedence, any sort of priority. And so the laborious recitation of, say, the universities' names: if in one phrase we refer to "Sedge and Charter Mill", we immediately have to reverse this in the rather tiresome and pathetic avoidance of notional favouritism and add, "Charter Mill and Sedge". Likewise "Tane, Chote" has urgently to be back-to-fronted, "Chote, Tane".'

'Oh, but come now, Elv, that is mere politesse, isn't it?' Theo Bastrolle (Business Studies) said. 'My parents told me about a weekly comic radio programme in the 1940s called *It's That Man Again* where one of the running jokes was a pair of characters about to pass through a door and saying, "After *you,* Claud." "No, after *you,* Cecil." Isn't the Sedge, Charter, Charter, Sedge and Chote, Tane, Tane, Chote like that?'

'It is deception. It is pretence,' Elvira replied. 'It is blind-eyeing.'

'In which respect, Elv?' Theo asked.

'You very kindly furnished us all with a copy of the centenary gig review in d'Brindle Hall, Theo,' she said. Elvira waved her copy. Other committee members studied theirs.

'Yes,' Theo replied.

'I'd like to ask the Chair – ask Martin – what kind of reception that review got at the time,' Elvira said. 'We are lucky to have someone who was well-placed in Sedge when so many of these events took place.'

'Reception?' Mart said. 'Receptions varied, like receptions of any opinion expressed in a newspaper.'

'How did *you,* personally regard it?' Elvira said.

'Regard exactly what, Elvira?' Mart said.

'Take this sentence about the *Tannhauser* interlude,' she replied, reading from her copy: '"As he clashed those two shining brass discs together at pretty well exactly the right dramatic moments one could see the challenging sound as defiance, a sort of Bronx cheer, aimed at those who regard his principalship as disastrous, and want him kicked out while there might still be time to save Sedge under a new chief and a more sane regime."' Elvira looked up from the article and gazed around the room, taking in everyone. 'Now, what do we make of that?' she asked.

'Well, what do *you* make of it, Elvira?' Martin replied, with a Claud and Cecil intonation. He wondered whether Elvira, also, had seen the historic tape of Charlie Drake half concussing himself with the cymbals din. He thought he could detect which way her questions were headed, though. He didn't want to be an accessory to bloodletting, and was glad to fall back on the excuse that a chair had to be all-round non-partisan. 'It's too long ago for me to remember what I felt then and I'm not allowed to have feelings now, except to exercise a casting vote if necessary, which it isn't.'

Elvira gave him a ten second you-fucking-fuckface stare then said, 'This is ridicule masquerading as praise, isn't it?' She waved the copy and returned to the text. 'We hear he did his banging bit at "pretty well exactly the right moments". What does "pretty well exactly" mean? It means not quite exactly. It is a boot in the balls phrased urbanely, but still a boot in the balls. To be slightly off with his cymbals contributions is as bad as being a mile off. It would rupture the *Tannhauser* excerpt.'

She lowered her eyes towards the end of the review then hopped about willy-nilly to make her points. 'He has charisma, yes, but no money to match it and make the charisma of some use. Childishly he can give a Bronx cheer but it damages nobody. "Red hat, no drawers" as the folk wisdom goes about mere show. Although Mart, for his own reasons, refuses to endorse this, the impression given in 1987 by the review is of a leader struggling frantically, pitiably, to lead, but barred from doing so any longer because he lacks the wherewithal. Almost everyone must have observed this. Mart, through what I suppose might be deemed respect for the conventions of his present role and a failure of memory, declines to say so, but probably knows that this is how things were.'

'You mustn't tell me what I'm thinking, Elvira,' Mart replied.

'And it is here that we come to the question of equality, and its relevance to the statues,' Elvira said.

'Relevant how?' Jed Laver (Industrial Relations) asked.

Theo said in a definitive, boardroom voice, 'What you're telling us, Elv, is that the review probably got the picture of Chote right, despite its snide tone here and there. You think he was generally regarded as a runaway nincompoop: massive, even glorious, ambitions, no genuine ability to achieve them. You believe this should not be tactfully, sentimentally, ignored, "blind-eyed" now. You think what would stick damningly in the reader's mind back then is the mention of his kennel of wild hatreds; and the notion that he should be kicked out and a new chief and more "sane" regime established while there was still time to save Sedge. Out of this analysis you would bring a demand that, in the matter of statues, Victor Tane's should, in some way or ways, indicate a superiority to Chote, Tane being the one who would soon have the task – and complete the task well – of repairing the appalling damage done by Lawford Chote.'

'Along those lines, Theo, yes,' Elvira said. 'This review offers vision. I'll say why it must have been effective. It's this: it has balance. Certainly it mocks his cymbals clumsiness, and is unkind in the *Titanic* comparison. But it also delivers admiration for him. It recognizes his inspired doggedness and positive imagination in creating d'Brindle Hall, a beautiful building and brilliantly acousticked concert centre. Jurbb saw that Chote refused to be domineered by money, or its shortage. Like some warrior hero he was facing fearful odds and *would* face them. But his defeat is treated as almost inevitable. The fearful odds are justifiably, accurately, fearful. He is blatantly unable to handle the basic task – running Sedge, or saving Sedge by the time O.T.O. wrote.'

'We still don't know who this Jurbb, capable of so many penetrating insights, really was, do we?' Angela said. 'Mart has admitted he can't help on this.'

'Jurbb is – or, at least was – Jurbb, as far as I could discover. I did wonder about the then local editor, Alan Norton-Hord, possibly choosing to hide under a pen-name, but that was only speculation,' Martin replied.

'He/she is by-lined as Music Correspondent. Did she/he review in the paper regularly?' Angela asked.

'Not to my knowledge,' Martin said.

'Those extraordinary initials,' Upp said.

'If they *are* initials,' Bill Davey said.

'How do you mean, Bill?' Lucy asked.

'We spoke of anagrams previously, taking up all the letters,' Davey said. 'The O.T.O. would be part of the hidden name – Jo Burbot, Rob Jobut. We called them "names to conjure with". Well, we've tried to conjure and the trick doesn't work.'

Elvira took charge again. 'Theo, with his business expertise, will be able to confirm what I'm going to say now. In management there is a theory dubbed The Peter Principle. Its originator argues that people in top jobs will frequently get promoted to a position one stage above their abilities. A vast muck-up results. Nixon would be an example, and Anthony Eden. And Lawford Chote. I gather that he had a brilliant academic and administrative career before Sedge. I wholly accept this. His CV must have been irresistible. But past form is only that – past. Sedge turned out to be a fatal bit too much for him. He valiantly, foolishly, made his wager against those fearful odds and lost, though unwilling to admit he'd lost until compelled to by the Universities Finance Centre. Happily, though, this, was not the end of the game. Someone else – Victor Tane – stepped in and ultimately secured recovery.'

'"A second Adam to the fight and to the rescue came," Upp said. 'Cardinal Newman?'

'Doesn't this rescue require special, obvious recognition?' Elvira replied. 'In universities we do not champion equality, and we certainly do not champion flagrant failure, nor the purblind determination not to acknowledge that failure, causing further chaos. We are *higher* education, in fact, the highest. We are the top, and this implies there is much below. We exist to recognize and encourage merit. There are First Class degrees and there are Third Class degrees. There are first class institutions. There are seventh or tenth class institutions. There are staff who get elected to the Royal Society. And there are others who don't. It would be dishonest and intellectually sloppy and perverse to pretend that each ex-principal deserves exactly the same quality memorial and similar prominence. We must have distinctions. That's what I've been getting at today.'

'What about the plinths?' Upp asked.

'Plinths are important, though not of the essence,' Elvira replied. 'But, yes, it might be appropriate to differentiate statues' status by plinth variations.'

'Plinths are very eloquent in their own stony way,' Angela said.

'Perhaps at that interesting contribution we should break,' the chair said.

TWENTY-FOUR

1987

Eligible under a special civil service protocol, Mart was invited to join them when Geraldine Fallows and Neddy Lane-Hinkton travelled from London to Sedge for a meeting with Lawford Chote in his suite there. Neddy had telephoned Martin in advance to tell him of the arrangements. 'Geraldine remains very anxious, Mart. Well, "anxious"? Perhaps that's not the word. It makes Geraldine sound nervy, which she ain't. Perhaps "watchful" would be more like it. Yes, very watchful.

'We had this Volvo pic, with its unclear, possibly disquieting implications; and now our press cuttings service here have put the O.T.O. Jurbb piece in front of her. They've been asked to look out for anything to do with Sedge and, or Charter Mill. You'll have seen the article, of course. *Jurbb* – who the fuck is he or she with a name like that? Sounds like a belch. Is it a misprint? We've done all the searches, but nix, Mart. And those initials. Is that another misprint? Should it be Otto? Are the sub-editors all pissed on that paper? We wondered if it was a real name anagrammed as cover. But we got only Jo Burbot, who'd be female, and Rob Jobut or Bob Rojto. Nothing on these, either.

'You'd have been at the concert, I imagine. Did you see anyone who looked like a Jurbb? Is that an absurd question? Probably. But what I mean is, he or she could be foreign. Possibly Jurbb is as commonplace as Smith in some other country. She or he might be black. There are probably some good music colleges over there in Africa, say, Malawi or Kenya. He or she could have been trained at one of those and then come to Britain looking for journo work. Music is very international. Just think of Aaron Copeland or Edith Piaf. There is often some quite interesting ethnic hullabaloo stuff on the BBC

Radio Three programme late at night. Would someone like that know *Convergence Of The Twain,* though? It's unquestionably a bit of a puzzler, Mart.

'Perhaps he or she at the concert, white or black, would be making notes to remind herself/himself of the *Titanic* witticism, and of Chote off-kilter on the cymbals. She or he possibly had one of those small torches used by theatre critics in the stalls when jotting down her/his reactions to the acting and sets. I wonder if you observed any little gleams like that?

'The *Titanic* stuff: that's savagery against Chote, and perhaps partly justified, but, it smears Geraldine as well, doesn't it? Smears all of us in her bailiwick. Implies negligence, indifference. Chote's ship is going down while Geraldine and her department busy ourselves elsewhere with flimflam. I mean she's our expert on university finances, and we're talking serious finance here, aren't we? As I remember it, there's a sea-worm in that poem excitedly waiting in the depths for a look at itself in one of the state room mirrors. This is a dark fate for a fine vessel. Not a pretty comparison, Mart.

'Ger didn't object to his staging the centenary concert – or, at least, she didn't object at full Geraldinish whack. Sedge is Sedge and to date still there, occupying its ground, educating its intakes, offering places for next year. She considered it reasonable for the birthday to be marked, despite everything. There's a sensitive side to Ger, not always on view, though. But then this fucking O.T.O. Jurbb is let loose on the event. We did inquiries and found that the editor of the paper is . . . hang on . . . I've got the name and details here . . . yes, the editor is an Alan Norton-Hord who was actually an undergrad at Sedge and held student union office. Him? Or him a party to it, although, plainly, he can't be anagrammed into Jurbb?

'But Ger says she thinks she divines a woman's hand and mind in the review. Don't ask me why – something to do with the use of adverbs, I gather. Geraldine's sharp. The fact that the initials are the same if read from the front or back like the word "kayak", infuriates her, more than the double "b" in Jurbb, though it's a near run thing, as Wellington said after Waterloo. She asks, what kind of parents would send a kid out into life with initials like those? It's an invitation to mockery and bullying, in her opinion. That is, if the O.T.O. Jurbb name is genuine. You're a prof. Have you ever heard of a word ending in a double b?'

'It's not the kind of thing that would come up in English Literature studies, or American. There's Bob Cratchit in *A Christmas Carol* where there are two "b"s and one is at the end, but it's separated from the earlier "b" by the "o",' Mart said.

'We might imagine that boob would be given two, with the round, base bit of the "b"s imitating a pair of knockers,' Neddy replied, 'but not so. Why is the second one necessary in Jurbb? No, not "necessary". That's my whole point. "Indulged in" rather than necessary. Utterly *un*necessary. The pronunciation is the same whether it's double or single. Geraldine is not against double "b"s *per se*. Clearly, she sees them as acceptable and even obligatory within the body of words like "Scrabble", and "rubble" and "babble." A single "b" in these instances would produce a different and possibly confusing pronunciation: "Scrabble" would sound like "Srayble", "rubble" like "rouble", "babble" like "babel". Sorry, Mart, am I, as it were, babbling on a bit? But for the repeated "b"s to be tacked on to the end, as in Jurbb, Geraldine regards as a kind of affront to readers of the paper and to all those associated with Sedge.

'Ger can see that the review might in a devious way be trying to support Sedge by lobbing some praise at Chote for getting the d'Brindle done, an acoustics paradise. ("Lobbing", there's another allowable double "b"! It would be the alternative "o" pronunciation if only one "b": lobing, maybe to mean earholing, eavesdropping.) Geraldine believes that Chote's enemies – the iceberg, metronomes, accountants, bailiffs, ministries – are depicted as evil persecutors of a decent, conscientious chap, if, admittedly rather headstrong. But she doubts whether this is the message most people will carry away from O.T.O., or may we call you O?

'Geraldine thinks there'd better be some head-to-head stuff – her head and Lawf's. She's talked to Tane, so has one side of the situation fairly clear; and she doesn't think it would be wise to wait for you to report back after my visit and our conclave at The Lock Gate. That was to ask you to keep us briefed. She doesn't believe there's time for this any longer.

Urgency has taken over. She possibly thinks, too, that you might not feel comfortable about offering insights on Chote because you have a certain admirable loyalty. Maybe she's right. I haven't heard anything from you since our lunch, and neither has she.'

Neddy paused, apparently hoping Mart would comment – attempt an explanation. He stayed silent, though. He supposed he *did* have a sort of loyalty to Chote off-and-on, even if he thought Chote often ludicrously and perilously wrong. Things were too complicated to be dealt with in this phone session with Neddy. And, anyway, Mart didn't feel like putting himself into a situation where he was offering excuses to someone like Ned, who had no boss status over him. Neddy had been a good lunch companion. This was the whole story.

Lane-Hinkton said, 'But she hasn't a down on you, Martin, because of your possible unwillingness to give us insider glimpses. She understands that you possibly don't wish to spy – to turn informant. Perhaps you consider that kind of thing contemptible. Regardless, she would like you to sit in along with myself when she sees Lawford. This will be what's known in our splendidly astute bureaucracy as a "Preparatory Parameters Survey (U)" the U standing not for Upper Class as usual in terms like "non-U", meaning prole, but for "Unminuted".

'The natty convention is that the two main, official figures – here, Geraldine Fallows and Lawford Chote – confer directly, armchair to armchair, or across a desk. But, so as to establish the meeting's informality and casual nature, two other people should be present, each linked to one of these chief partici-pants, though having no designated connection with the topic or topics discussed; in this case, you, Martin, and myself. You're an academic, not an administrator, more interested in Pinter than in policy; and I am only a sort of Premier League office boy and gofer at Universities Finance Centre. The essen-tial nobodies – that's us. But we are both allowed to join discussions – are not mere clerkly background, on call with appropriate stats and bottled water. In fact we are *required* to join in. However, the meeting or meetings has, have, no execu-tive power because of our non-executive role in it, them. By contributing we invalidate. Think of the crazy, impregnable logic in Joseph Heller's famous novel, *Catch 22*. The rules and conventions for these "unminuted" sessionss are not quite up to that mad standard, but let's say they form a *Catch Twenty-One-And-A-Half*. The reasoning Byzantine but almost flawless. A meeting of this sort might not get known about except to those involved. But even if it does, never mind, because such get-togethers can be passed off as simply idle chin-wagging with no binding outcomes, full of sound and hooey, signifying nothing much.

'Geraldine is especially agitated by the closing Jurbb thought, Mart.' Neddy spoke at his accustomed slow pace and Martin tried to guess which side of the mouth the talk was coming from. Mart thought that if he could get another hearing of a multi-syllabled word like 'agitated' he might be able to diagnose the left or right source. It wasn't vital to know, but would help Mart keep Neddy's jolly type of face in his mind, bringing some lightness to a fairly clunking conversation so far.

'Did you say "agitated", Neddy?' he asked

'Yes, agitated.'

Mart found he could visualize this word laid out like a patient etherized upon a table and, looking hard at it, as a surgeon might, felt it was most probably from Neddy's lips angled for ouput from the left. This verdict was instinct only. Mart realized that. He couldn't have pointed to any evidence, but he would have bet a bundle it was left. It came to him as a kind of revelation.

'Charisma, Mart,' Neddy said. 'The sort of pay-off for the review, a conclusive thumbs up.'

'Charisma *is* mentioned, at the end, yes.'

'What especially troubles Geraldine and probably persuaded her to decide on a personal trip to Sedge and Lawford, is the yoking together of Sedge and Chote's charismas, or should it be charismae?'

'Yoking?'

'I have the final sentence in front of me, Mart. "Although Sedge and Lawford Chote are perilously short of cash they still have charisma."'

'Yes, that's the last line.'

'I think you'll see why this would disturb Geraldine. Perhaps, in fact, it's already troubled *you*.'

'In which respect, Ned?'

'You don't see it?'

'See what?'

'The identification charisma-wise of Sedge and Chote.'

'Identification?'

'The marriage – the assumption as Geraldine sees it, and as I'm inclined to see it myself, I admit . . . yes, the assumption seems to be that they are interdependent for charisma – if one of them has it then the other must, too. Now, Mart, Sedge obviously does have charisma. It is a university 100 years old which, although by comparison with Oxbridge or the Sorbonne might seem trivial, is *not* trivial for provincial, red-brick and breeze-block places.

'And Sedge has alumni in distinguished posts right across the main professions, in business and the creative arts. True, Charter Mill has an international goalkeeper among its most successful former students, who's probably earning more than any Sedge graduate – and three times more than the Charter Mill principal's and senior academics' combined salaries. But we are not talking loot here, are we, Mart? We are not talking goalkeepers. We are talking intellectual renown earned over the decades. We are talking genuine charisma. The danger, as Geraldine views it, and I don't disagree, is that Lawford, being of the awkwardly indomitable, egomaniac kind we know him to be, will decide that if Sedge has charisma, the principal running Sedge at present, i.e., Lawf, must also have charisma. Geraldine fears, and I share this apprehension, she fears that Chote, on reading O.T.O. Jurbb, will deduce that all he has to do is carry on as ever in his job because the way he conducts this has brought him charisma and will continue doing so after a few local difficulties about money and debt have been dealt with and forgotten, just as the inept cymbals interlude will be. He's not going to kowtow to accountants and their talk of black holes in the Sedge account books. His view is that charisma will cancel all those piddling anxieties.'

'"Tax not the royal saint with vain expense",' Mart said.

'"High-heaven rejects the lore/Of nicely calculated less or more",' Neddy replied. 'But there's another aspect to it.'

'I *did* wonder.'

'It could be that some harsh things will be said at this meeting and some harsh decisions confirmed. Although Geraldine can be very understanding and sweet-tempered, clearly she isn't coming on a crisis trip from London by train just to dispense understanding and sweet-temper. It's true she sees my expenses sheets, of course, so is aware of our pleasant, refreshing snack at The Lock Gate, and might feel it worth a visit. She wanted to know if it was up to snuff – can't believe any eatery outside London is a goer – and I naturally referred to the black-pudding hash. But I don't think this, on its own, accounts for her determination to travel. For all I know, Mart, she isn't into black-pudding hash. She didn't indicate one way or t'other.

'In any case, she'll probably want to lunch in the Sedge staff dining room. She's heard of the lavish upgrading and might feel a duty to look at it and the deluxe carpeted approach. No, the black-pudding hash is probably not a motivator. She has a well-defined, serious purpose. This is why I spoke of possible harshness arising. The meeting will begin, most likely, in a very civilised, even amiable, style. In fact, Geraldine would see this as essential. It ties in, Mart, with another reason for wanting you present. If matters reach an abusive, end-of-the-fucking-road, ultimatum stage, Ger will require someone present who can report to the rest of the Sedge staff that Lawford was given every consideration and kindness from the outset but would offer no concessions, no decent response; behaved, in fact, as if he were in a morality play representing the quality of pig-headedness. She wants head-to-head contact but not with a pig.

'This is where you'll be invaluable, Mart. Colleagues know that you and Lawford are friends, and if you have to admit he behaved in a negative, blatantly uncooperative style they will accept this as almost certainly a fair and honest judgement. Geraldine or myself might be suspected of bias. She has to keep in mind that even when the Sedge situation has finally settled she will still need workable relations with Sedge and all of Britain's universities, never mind what shape Sedge emerges in after these troubles. She will not want to be regarded as a bureau-cratic bully. Such a reputation would spread far and fast. It might appear that having kicked her way through what is known as the glass ceiling, hindering women from reaching a major job, she'd developed the kicking habit and had given some toecap to Lawford when he was down – though Lawford would never have admitted he was down, of course. Down is not his habitat.'

'You spoke of an ultimatum, Neddy,' Martin said.

'Oh, yes, there could be an ultimatum.'

'Of what nature?'

'Geraldine is sure to bring documents already part prepared, in case. She wouldn't necessarily produce them. She probably wouldn't *want* to produce them. She'd prefer another route. But that route might not be open. It would be a matter of judgement at the time.'

'Documents for what?'

'We're talking *aide memoires*.'

'Are we?'

'This is one of the things about Geraldine – preparedness: she's famed for it. Geraldine could have mentored Lord Baden-Powell, founder of the scout movement with its motto, "Be prepared",' Neddy replied. 'I've had her a few times as you'd expect and she makes all the arrangements – no possibility of discovery and interruption; champagne, vintage brut from an ice box; cork double-thumbed out by her in one explosive, decisive move and jetting off to some safe corner of the room or car or garden shed; the wine poured at exactly the right angle into the flutes, preserving the liveliness, but with no wasteful and messy bubbling over the sides and perhaps chillingly on to her body; biting only in areas normally hidden by garments; the cork recovered afterwards by Ger and disposed of in a public waste bin with the bottle and any of its paper-bag shreds so as to leave no evidence of a high-jinks, multi-cum occasion.'

'Preparedness to do with the ultimatum?' Martin replied.

'The documents ready for close interrogation if utilized. Not for signature yet, obviously. No signed agreements can come out of a Preparatory Parameters Survey (U), because the meeting has no power or acknowledged status: might not even be known about generally. It is irrevocably (U). The procedure she'd be hoping for is discussion involving all four parties – herself, Chote, you, me; verbal agreement on the required major points;

agreement, also, on the date of a formal, officially diaried meeting; signatures, then; minutes then. No invitation for us this time because our presence in an apparently policy-making session would disqualify its proceedings and render the signatures worthless.'

'Agreement on what, Ned?'

'The terms would have been set out in the *aide memoire* I mentioned, but need not be referred to, let alone shown, if the parties at the (U) settle everything by conversation and hand-shakes. The pattern for this would be each of us shakes hands with the other three, although, technically, the handshakes you and I provide would add up to bugger-all, especially as one of the handshakes would be *between* you and me, who have utterly no rank, and so whose handshake rates as bugger-all squared. The handshake between Lawford and Geraldine would also amount to bugger-all at that stage since the meeting had no standing because you and I were there, Mart.

'However, the Lawford–Geraldine handshake will – if it happens – be of a promissory kind, resting on the honour of the two. She'd be entirely willing to accept this commitment from Chote, although unbacked by paperwork at that juncture. I've heard Geraldine call him by all kinds of abusive, filthy and blasphemous terms, but I have also heard her pronounce him straight – straight in the sense of undevious and trustworthy, not anything to do with sexuality.'

'But what would she and he be shaking hands *about*, Neddy? What would the *aide memoire*, if ever brought forward, aid them to remember?' Mart replied.

'I don't think this sounds anti-woman, but to treat a handshake as something more or less sacred we would normally take as being between males, I believe, wouldn't you say so, Mart? But for Geraldine, who has kicked her way through the glass ceiling, this, in a heartening way, seems to free up her hands as well as her feet so she can get in on the shake procedure, as if it were absolutely normal for females. But she certainly remains all woman, Mart. I can assure you she won't black mark you for seeming to be very much of Chote's inner gang. Are you keen on brut champagne at all? I can't recall what we sipped at The Lock Gate.'

'You ought to keep an *aide memoire*, Neddy.'

'And the biting, although forceful, is nicely controlled to draw no blood; perhaps more a suck with tooth backing rather than an authentic bite,' Lane-Hinkton said. 'The redness soon fades but, obviously, for a day or two you have to be careful when undressing at home or with someone else. This is only standard decent manners.'

TWENTY-FIVE

1987

'Thank you, thank you, thank you!' Victor Tane yelled. He waved graciously to the crowd of spectators lining the pavement. It was the kind of wave he'd seen performed by a Caesar to the masses in a film on TV lately, probably *Ben-Hur*. The imperiousness of it didn't quite fit in with all the thank yous. Caesars wouldn't lavish gratitude on their subjects. But Tane wasn't a Caesar and thought he'd better go half-and-half: part grand and aloof, part affable and populist.

Although skinny, he had a big, refined voice, the sort of voice you might hear if the colonel himself were commanding a Coldstream guard of honour for some visiting head of state. A jazz band banged brassily away fairly near in the procession but Victor could be heard above it. He was standing on the back of a slow-moving, open lorry. 'Thank you for supporting our charities,' he shouted. Students in a range of comic costumes and masks – Bo-Peep, Red Riding Hood, Cruella de Vil, Micky Mouse, Oliver Hardy with a padded stomach, small moustache, braces, black bowler – they moved among the bystanders with collecting boxes. 'Give, give, give!' Tane bellowed. 'It's Bounty Week.'

'Yes, folk, be generous. Dig deep,' Bernard Optor shouted. He had a big voice, too, and was built for it. He'd have had plenty of practice, cursing referees or his defensive backs for mistakes that left him exposed. He was alongside Tane, wearing the usual kit when in goal for his club or country: navy woollen bobble hat, polo-necked green sweater, brown woollen mittens, navy shorts, football boots. Behind him, reduced size imitation goal posts with netting had been rigged up on the lorry. His bulk would have made it more or less impossible to get a ball past him into that net.

Tane himself had on a yellow-and-black striped football shirt. Ursula said it made him look like a tall wasp. He wore also a blue ski hat, black shorts and red-and-white trainers. He was a good deal over six feet in height, slight and gawky, bordering on the wispy. He'd known he wasn't at his best in sports gear, or any gear involving shorts, but Optor had phoned a while ago to say he'd thought of a way to help Tane and Charter Mill, and Victor had agreed to his scheme. His scheme required shorts.

Tane's acceptance of the plan was in some sense posthumous kow-towing to his mother, her orders unspoken and, in fact, non-existent, of course, but envisaged as very true to her character, if only she'd been alive: *'Victor, cherish, heed and obey this glorious goalkeeper.'* From his days as an undergraduate at Charter, Optor apparently remembered the traditional Bounty Week, when the two universities put on a combined carnival parade through the city centre to raise money for a handful of charities. Optor had said, 'We'll do a footy theme for one of the lorries, eh, Principal? But I suppose I can call you Victor now, or even Vic, after so many years and since we're buddies, but it does feel cheeky.' Optor explained the ins and outs of the project and said he'd 'pop over' from Spain to take part.

He'd told Tane his agent, Loriner Vone, was vastly enthusiastic about it. Vone had said that such a pure, unmaterialistic labour of love carefully publicized was worth its weight in pounds sterling or the equivalent in pesetas, i.e., numerically a lot more. He didn't think he'd ever come across a smarter PR gambit. Not just the local media would be interested but national, too – the great Bernard Optor journeying back to his *alma mater* on a good, utterly selfless mission; loyalty of a magnificently high order. Vone considered this was the kind of generous gesture guaranteed to help improve the general reputation and image of professional soccer. It would consolidate the link with the game's fans, help build a fine relationship with them, almost certainly pushing up attendances. In particular, this example of the 'sweeter' and 'more wholesome' aspect of players' behaviour off the pitch might encourage more women to support the game. The extra following for Optor and his club would, naturally, be reflected in fatter transfer fees if he moved in the future. Although Optor played for a Spanish team the favourable impact of his Bounty Week contribution would certainly reach the media there as well as throughout the UK and pile more value on to Bernie.

Charter Mill would not be called on to pay any of the costs for Optor's travel, accommodation and other expenses, Optor told Tane. Vone had explained to Bernie that such outlay could be set against tax because the benevolent, spontaneous gesture by him in supporting Charter Mill would be very germane, if not essential, to developing his celebrity profile as not just a soccer star but a citizen who cared in a positive, practical, deep style about the community. He wasn't someone who simply stood between the sticks blocking or fisting out balls. He shone with responsibility in the widest of contexts. Loriner had said this could be deftly yet sensitively utilized.

Bernie told Tane that Loriner Vone believed the 'community concept' was an infallible switch-on for the media, national and local, and the kind of coverage Optor would get was sure to be a plus, both for himself and 'the education place in question'. And for the charities. People in Whitehall would be impressed by Optor's obvious splendidly strong bond with the past 'education place in question' because it proved that this 'education place in question' was brilliant. Optor had said he might be able to bring one or two other famous footballers with him to boost the lorry's cast.

And Optor had, in fact, brought a couple of top players – Pierre Pajot and Sean Nuseby, both in club gear. Their expenses, also, would be an allowable tax break for Optor. On the back of the lorry now they mimicked shots at Optor's goal and all three of them frequently bent over the sides of the vehicle to sign autograph books of fans who trotted to keep pace while Optor and his friends scribbled. Although Tane had felt obliged to get into soccer kit himself to maintain tone, he didn't expect anyone to want *his* autograph.

It was part of the Bounty Week tradition that both principals should be personally involved in the cavalcade and a little way ahead, next in line to the jazz lorry, Victor could see Lawford Chote apparently garbed in breastplate armour and occasionally wielding a sword. He was clearly meant to be Shakespeare's Macbeth. He wore a pink plastic crown. Near him three staff members dressed and made-up as witches sat around a big metal cauldron that simmered over a paraffin heater. It gave off occasional puffs of steam. Most probably the witches would be muttering their creepy spells, though Tane could not hear any of that from this distance. Would they predict for Lawford what was going to happen to Sedge and Charter? The early witches' scene in *Macbeth* had a mewing brindled cat referred to. Maybe Chote would see some sort of link to the d'Brindle Hall. Which sort, though?

Victor thought one of the witches might be Chote's Volvo companion, now in rags, his face smeared with what could be black boot polish, and with a wig made of what seemed to be a mixture of grimy cord and rope bits.

TWENTY-SIX

1987

As the Sedge *Macbeth* float trundled the last stage of its journey, Chote seemed to get bored with the play-acting. He sheathed the plastic sword in its glinting plastic scabbard and put it on the floor. He came and squatted down with the witches at the cauldron and said to Martin, 'So what kind of future do you see, Third Witch? "If you can look into the seeds of time/And say which grain will grow and which will not?" We see her tactics, don't we, Mart?'

'Whose?'

'Geraldine's.'

'Tactics?'

'There's to be a meeting, isn't there – Geraldine, Lane-Hinkton, you, me? Why does she require you in on it? I'll tell you: she's trying to concoct an appearance of fairness. Geraldine's bringing Lane-Hinkton for various services, so she'll balance that by inviting you. She wouldn't want, say, Roy Gormand with me. He's near the end and seeks a calm and sedate life from now on. Entirely understandable. He would do his customary act of backing me absolutely on whatever, wherever – not so much loyalty as serfdom. She believes that wouldn't be so with you, Mart. The main part of your career is still to come, isn't it? You'd like Sedge to survive in its present state to help you along with that. Also entirely under-standable, Mart. Geraldine believes she and Lane-Hinkerton can convince you that what they're going to propose is the correct and, in fact, the *only* feasible policy for Sedge. She's sure they can win you over and sure, also, that you will then help them to persuade me into cooperation with them. Blandishments – you'll get blan-dishments, and they'll expect you to give *me* blandishments. It's why I ask how you see the future, Mart. Will they be able to recruit you?'

'Ned Lane-Hinkton phoned and spoke of an ultimatum, but didn't specify what it was,' Martin Moss replied.

'Oh, I can tell you: they'll demand I cut Sedge expenditure for at least a spell of years. "Do it our way or we slash all government funds to Sedge immediately. You wouldn't be able to pay the staff or put the lights on."'

'That would be extreme, wouldn't it?' Mart replied.

'Geraldine *is* extreme when she wants to be. Lane-Hinkerton would copy. She's his boss, *inter alia*.' Chote waved to some spectators and adjusted his breastplate which seemed to be giving him discomfort. He became silent, head bent forward a little. Mart went quiet, too.

Second Witch, Jasper Dunning (Archaeology), and often a deep-dyed nuisance, said, '"Stay you imperfect speakers, tell me more." That's a Macbeth line, but Witch 2 has borrowed it.'

'Sod off, Jasper,' Chote replied.

'You mentioned the future, I think, Principal,' Dunning said.

'Yes, the future for Sedge, now, starting at 1987 and going on into the 1990s and eventually into the new millennium as far as we can see,' Chote said. '2001, 2010, 2020 etcetera.'

'But you've pissed on that, haven't you, Principal? Never

mind the new millennium and thereafter. Is Sedge going to reach even the start of the 1990s so my students can get their degrees?'

'There are more important matters than one year's student degrees,' Chote said. They were talking to each other across the cauldron, the steam blotting out one face for a while, then the other.

'My classes don't think there are more important things than their degrees,' Dunning said.

'I've worked to make places available for many more students to get their degrees,' Chote replied.

'And you've made a fucking mess of it, Chote. You're going to sink Sedge solo.'

Chote stood. He picked up the scabbard and sword and moved fast around the cauldron towards Dunning.

TWENTY-SEVEN

2014

Theo said, 'Before the break Elvira was talking about the need to put a precise, personal value on each of the two principals, not simply and tritely regard them as equals. She suggested that any difference in worth – and she saw a mighty difference – yes, this difference should be reflected in the debate about statues. It means we've had a pair of very fundamental proposals before us lately. First came Wayne's outright, even sweeping, declaration that there should be no statues at all, because many would consider such memorials elitist, backward-looking, stonily lifeless while pretending to be alive. I think the word "naff" was also used, though I wouldn't like to attempt a definition. Wayne's submission was, of course, well-expressed and structured, but not favoured by this group.

'Elvira's subsequent claim that it is intellectually slipshod and even dishonest to treat both principals as of the same merit, and that Victor Tane's statue should somehow indicate this, is almost as deeply challenging. I don't believe she would go so far as to say that there should be only one statue – Tane's – though some might think this is where her argument must lead.

Bill Davey said, 'It surely would. What occurred in 1987 was a crisis involving two universities and two principals. One of those universities was in real danger of disintegration because – it could be convincingly argued – yes, because of the policies followed by one of those principals, Lawford Chote. But, absolute disaster was prevented, and here we are today in a healthy, distinguished university formed from the merged Charter Mill and Sedge, or Sedge and Charter Mill. One of those two principals was hugely influential and, indeed, instrumental, in bringing about the 1987 rescue act: Victor Tane.

'Suppose we went along with Elvira's premise, there would plainly be something absurd, in the full, philosophical, chaotic universe, sense of that term, if the architect of catastrophe – Chote – were commemorated at all, let alone in some statue inferior to Tane's. Could any sculptor indicate in his/her works that one principal had been a wondrous, resourceful saviour while the other was a bonkers, money-chucking, fuck-up, though well-intentioned?'

'It might be possible to get statues from two separate artists, one specialising in happy, ebullient-seeming likenesses, the other in those less happy and ebullient,' Angela replied.

'*Yellow Pages*?' Jed asked. '"Jolly Statues Ltd. Monumental Cheeriness. At Your Personal Service." Or "Morose Statues, Free, Miserable Home Delivery in the UK".'

'Tane's scrimshank, spectral body-form wouldn't easily be made to appear ebullient,' Gordon Upp said.

'I want to bring to the meeting some other archive material unearthed in my searches,' Theo replied. 'It might have a bearing on our present discussions. Well, no "might" – it *does*, certainly have a bearing. There was then, in 1987, as there is now, in 2014, a Bounty Week devoted to raising funds for charities. The 1987 Bounty Week turned out to be exceptional because a famous soccer goalkeeper, Bernard Optor, plus two other international footballers, appeared with Victor Tane on one of the Charter Mill floats in the annual motorized parade. Archive papers show that Optor was a Charter Mill graduate. He must have dutifully come back to give Tane and Charter some *réclame* at a critical time, and it worked.'

'Bernie Optor?' Gordon Upp said. 'Played most of his club soccer in Spain? Wasn't he involved in a let-goals-in-for-a-fee scandal?'

'Later,' Theo replied. 'In 1987 he was close to sainthood. Because of Optor and his pals the Bounty Week back then got a lot of press coverage, national as well as local.' He brought copies of some newspaper cuttings from his briefcase and put them on the table to be passed around. 'Most of the attention is on the three players, and particularly Optor. You'll see pictures of young kids scampering alongside the lorry to get autographs. In the background one can spot Victor Tane in soccer gear – a yellow-and-black striped jersey.'

'He looks like a tall wasp,' Lucy Lane said.

'There'd obviously been a decision to pick soccer as this float's theme and attract publicity for Tane and Charter. Note the imitation goal posts and netting to Victor's left. The aim evidently was to make Charter and its head look successful, strong, popular at that time of massive tension in the city's universities. Optor is praised in all the papers for faithfully taking time to help his *alma mater*. There must have been a briefing to let reporters know he'd graduated from Charter Mill. This was a skilfully planned operation. The media had been managed. Soccer agents would be very experienced at that.

'For fairness, the Sedge main float also got mentions, but usually well down the columns. Chote was there apparently as Macbeth with breastplate, sword and dagger at his belt, and, no doubt, the occasional warlike scowl.'

'I was a witch,' Martin said. 'We made up some curses about Charter Mill to chant and boiled murky water in a big metal tub to give off sinister fumes.'

'There are several interesting paragraphs about that,' Theo said. He read from one of the cuttings. '"When the Sedge float was passing through Highbridge Road a fight seemed to break out on the back of the lorry between Chote and one of the witches, a man but supposed to be female. Eyewitnesses said Macbeth had put his sword away in its scabbard earlier as if tired of the game, but there was what looked like a heated

conversation between him and one of the witches, and suddenly
he picked up the sword, still in its scabbard, moved fast around
the cauldron, and began to beat the witch with it.

'The witch had on only Y-fronts and a sort of in-character,
unfetching sleeveless smock, probably made from old potato
sacks. Although the weapon used by Macbeth was only plastic,
it could most likely give quite painful blows on the witch's
poorly protected body. The witch didn't defend himself very
well, as if shocked and confused by this onslaught. As a tip-top
warrior, Macbeth was sure to know the value of surprise."'

Theo said, 'The writer leaves straight reporting and does
some speculation now. "But, while Macbeth was naturally
capable of such very sudden physical aggression, nobody
expected it from the principal of a university. Macbeth would
have been proud of Lawford Chote – the sword hidden away
until the exactly proper moment. Some of those watching this
burst of violence couldn't decide whether it was a real dispute
or something staged – what used to be called 'a happening' to
amuse spectators.

'"Red weals and dark bruising could be seen on the witch's
neck and shoulder, though, which should have proved to spectators that it must be a genuine in-house spat. The witches' bowl
or cauldron was tipped over during this fracas and some people
watching got soaked, perhaps scalded, by the hot, filthy water.
Several men shouted curses and for a while it looked as if they
might get aboard the float and hammer Chote and possibly the
witches, though the witches couldn't really be blamed for the
mishap. None of this was derived from the play. Shakespeare's
Macbeth never attacked a witch or witches with his sword,
either in its scabbard or not; and the witches' cauldron was not
spilled, it just went on simmering."'

'It wasn't you he went for, was it, Mart?' Lucy asked.

'No, Second Witch. I was Third. The episode lasted only a
minute and a half. Some of it made the local TV news. Lawford
apologized all round and offered to pay for any dry-cleaning
needed and/or ointment and painkillers for the folk scalded.'

'In some ways this must have made the whole attempt to
resemble the play hopeless,' Gordon Upp said. 'I mean, there'd
be no dry-cleaning available in those days, nor ointment, though

I think certain leaves were believed to have an analgesic influence.'

'Dry-cleaning and ointment were not needed in the play,' Elvira replied, 'because the cauldron stayed upright and bubbling OK with bits of all sorts in it – a thumb, a newt's eye, a dog's tongue, a lizard's leg. Probably they wouldn't have had any of those on the Sedge lorry, except for thumbs. And Macbeth didn't clobber one of the witches.'

'Macbeth gets terminated, doesn't he?' Jed asked. 'It's a tragedy, yes?'

'Some actors won't mention the play's name because the plot is so dark,' Wayne said.

'Fucking precious thesps,' Elvira replied.

'Yes, it's dark,' Theo said. 'Maybe that's why Chote picked this role. It's an aggressive-defensive, do-your-worst, kind of choice.'

'But what's your point about the statues or statue, Theo?' Upp said.

'What do we learn from this age-old, back-of-a-lorry, stuff?' Elvira asked.

'Well, Elvira, isn't there, on the face of it, a sort of equality, despite what you've just told us?' Theo asked. 'Both principals, were willing to make a spectacle of themselves for the charities' sake, each recognising the force of the Bounty Week tradition and cheerfully ready to uphold it. That is a very basic, very substantial, resemblance, as is the fact that they were both major scholars, whatever their qualities as managers might have been.

'However, I'd say that if we're going to put differing values on them the nobler, more worthwhile figure is Lawford, although we know he would tumble before the year ended. There's a magnificent, basically flawed grandeur to him, as there should be to all tragic heroes and heroines, or heroines and heroes, in the theatre. He stands alone with his plastic sword, dagger and breastplate and will confront whatever comes. Just like Macbeth at Dunsinane he wouldn't lose his nerve even if a forest started to move against him.'

'Why did he attack Second Witch, Mart?' Jed asked.

'Second Witch was a Sedge lecturer called Jasper Dunning (Archaeology), ever a troublesome, sniping sod, recently knighted for the quality of his digs in Wales and France. He said something Chote didn't like. I forget what now.'

'Lawford's reaction shows he wouldn't take any insult or insubordination,' Davey said.

'Staunch, as I've already pointed out,' Theo replied. 'I regard Tane as a lesser figure, who had to make use of help from elsewhere – from a supposed celebrity, and a tainted celebrity, as he would become subsequently. There are three time lines running in our discussion: 1987, now, but also the quarter of a century and some between. It's my conviction that there must be two statues. Tane's should have about it somehow a spruce aura of achievement, because his success in making the amalgamation possible is plain and undeniable. But there should be a hint that his success came via a dubious, meretricious route. Possibly the sculptor could get some shifty, conspiratorial quality into his eyes. Chote's statue should also have an aura, but of non-surrender, tenacity, valour and error – firmness in the face of those previously mentioned fearful odds; the fearful odds that refused to change in his favour and, in fact, grew worse.'

'You'd say we get a generous dose of catharsis from Lawford?' Lucy asked. 'Tragedy is supposed to bring that, isn't it?'

'I used to know what catharsis meant,' Upp said. 'Something emotional?'

'Release,' Elvira said.

'Yes, good,' Mart said, standing.

Theo began to gather up his cuttings, but remained sitting. 'A postscript, if you don't mind, Chair. It might have a bearing on the statues mission. In my search of the archives I found some very well maintained secretarial diaries. They were hand-written. Nowadays, of course, they'd be in some computer's memory bank. Normally, the entries give time and place of meetings and a short title of the business carried out, the names of those present, duration, and sometimes the outcome if a policy decision were reached. But I came across a May 1987 occasion in Chote's suite without any of the customary detail. The diary note said only: "Principal's conference area engaged from 1420 to 1647".

'The date could be significant. It's very close to the crux

stages of the Chote–Sedge crisis, isn't it? I had a really thorough hunt for anything further, particularly names of those who might have attended, and the subject for consideration. Nothing, though.'

Martin sat down again. 'Yes, this would have been a "Preparatory Parameters Survey (U)",' he said.

'Oh, what's that when it's at home?' Elvira replied.

'It's a meeting that existed, but also didn't,' Mart said. 'The bracketed U indicates the type of Preparatory Parameters Survey: the unminuted genre. There will be no list of those participating, no labelling title, no statement of results. It happens that I was at this one plus Geraldine Fallows – Baroness Fallows now – Neddy Lane-Hinkton and Lawford Chote. The fact that I, or rather Neddy and I, were included means that this session could not have taken place.'

'I don't get it,' Angela said.

'It's a beauty, isn't it?' Mart replied.

'But the diary reports that it *did* take place,' Lucy said.

'No, it says that the conference area was engaged for a measured period,' Mart said.

'Engaged with what, if it wasn't a meeting?' Wayne asked.

Mart said, 'What I was present at *felt* like a meeting – four people coming together to talk, two having travelled from London specifically to be there – but I was told with great firmness that reference to a meeting having taken place was perverse and foolishly deluded.'

Gordon Upp said, 'This reminds me of that nonsense poem by Hughes Mearns:

"Yesterday upon the stair
I met a man who wasn't there.
He wasn't there again today.
I wish, I wish, he'd go away."'

'But Martin *was* there,' Elvira said.

'And because I was it couldn't have taken place,' Mart said.

TWENTY-EIGHT

1987

'**G**ood legs,' Ursula Tane said.

Vic Tane didn't much like this. His own legs were not good – between bony and emaciated – and they'd been displayed on the Bounty Week float. 'Hell, Ursula, if I said that, but about a woman, you'd go into a flaming jealous spasm.'

'When a man praises a woman's legs he's not really thinking about the legs but where they start from or lead up to, and how welcoming they would be when apart. A woman's legs might be lovely, but they are not the complete agenda.'

Ursula had lovely legs, but Tane would admit they were not the complete agenda.

'Whereas,' she told him, 'when I note Lawford Chote's "good legs" it just means what it says, legs that seem strong and well shaped. Normally, his legs wouldn't be on show, but when he's doing a Macbeth in breastplate over short jerkin, there they are, bare and obviously serviceable.'

They were watching the late evening local TV news coverage of the Bounty Week parade, and Chote's sudden, all-out, frenzied attack with his scabbarded sword on one of the witches. The film showed most of the tussle including the tip-up of the cauldron, dowsing some onlookers with what looked like very mucky water. They were obviously cursing and threatening Chote and the witch, but viewers needed to lip-read because the sound had been edited out on grounds of hygiene.

Vic Tane adored television. They had four sets in Kule House, the eighteenth-century, semi-rural, six-bedroomed mansion that came with the job at Charter Mill. It had been already furnished but Tane added more. This signalled a kind of compulsion. They were in what was called the East Study where the largest TV stood, a very over-furnished, small room.

As well as the television it contained a three-piece suite of two ample easy chairs and a lengthy settee in pale mauve velveteen, a sideboard, a round, rosewood table, two nests of small mahogany tables, an archery target on its stand for use in the grounds fairly often when Ursula and Victor competed against each other, Victor almost always the winner. This was important to him, even vital. Ursula could sometimes make Tane seem stupid in argument, but he had the drop on her as to bull's eyes. He would mock her: 'We'd never have won at Agincourt if our longbow troops were like you, Urs.' She liked this ugly shortening of her name because it sounded similar to the French for a female bear – *ourse* – and made her feel cuddlesome, like a teddy.

'The other two witches don't do anything to help their sister,' Ursula said. 'Poltroons. Where's solidarity?'

'Despite the rope wig and rough garments, I think I recognize one of them from a photograph taken a while ago, a non-witch picture. He was in Chote's Volvo then, not on the back of a lorry, and seemingly a new member of Lawford's special clique. He probably wouldn't side against Macbeth here.'

'He can't survive this,' Ursula said, pointing at the screen.

'Who? The witch? Lawford's sword and scabbard are only toys. The witch hits back. He's taking most of the blows on his arm.'

'Chote.'

'Survive it?'

'This publicity will finish him. I mean, Vic, this is the principal of a university. OK, a provincial university but still a university with a boss who ought to behave with some decorum. The police are sure to be involved and the safety people – antics on the back of a lorry and chucking hot water over what are known as innocent bystanders, that is, bystanders whose innocence means they don't need a wash, especially not in foul water. Was he drunk, or high on something? In a way it's hilarious, of course: a procession admirably in support of charities becomes a venue for thuggery.'

'But in a way it's also sad, of course,' Victor said.

'Has he flipped because of the Sedge troubles?'

'Flipped?'

'Overheated brain, trying to think of a way out of the Sedge agonies when there probably isn't one – or not one he could accept,' she replied. 'The only one he *would* accept, most probably, is Sedge's debts written off and a new tranche of Education Ministry boodle for him to squander.'

'I think the witch must have said something to him. They seemed to be chatting normally near the cauldron, the way any two people might chat near a witches' cauldron, and then abruptly he goes ape.'

'Said what?'

'Obviously, something offensive.'

'What sort of something?' she said.

'Oh, about Sedge and the mess he's made of it. They'd be doom-laden words and coming from a witch who, don't forget, Urs, has second-sight into the future.'

'It's not a witch, it's a bloke doing a turn for Bounty Week, as you did.'

'But Chote's in a bad state,' Victor replied.

'Pissed?

'Has strain made him deluded, so he can't tell the difference between street-theatre and fact, fantasy and the back of a lorry?' Victor found some of it unbearably embarrassing to watch and let his eyes wander from the screen and move around the East Study. What he liked about cramming so much furniture in was the way this corrected how things had been at home when he was a youngster. His mother and father were minimalists by nature, long before the word and style became commonplace. Some rooms in the house had only a couple of basic items in them, though they were used daily, not abandoned.

'Victor, I must have space!' his mother had bawled at him one day, when standing in the middle of what she and Tane's father referred to as the Nominal Room, because they'd gone in there during Mrs Tane's pregnancy to decide on what the coming child should be called. The room could offer then, as it probably could until the house was sold, two straight-backed kitchen chairs and an ottoman with a padded hinged lid where sheets were kept.

His mother had told Vic that she and his father sat opposite each other on the chairs for hours going through names.

Eventually they'd settled on Victor Horace, and Madge Emily for a girl. 'So you see, Victor Horace, what I mean when I state in all humility I must, absolutely *must*, have space,' his mother had said that day when he was in his teens, touching with a kind of awe and reverence the chair she'd been on when choosing Victor Horace and Madge Emily.

Vic Tane hadn't, in fact, seen why she should demand space because of the naming slog and to counter what he saw as the barminess of his mother's supposed logic he went in for loading rooms at Kule with gear so that he could prove to himself, and to anyone else who inquired, that he was not for ever bound by his mother's thinking, even though she and his father had spent so long in an uncomfortable, mean-looking room naming him and the girl who didn't come.

Tane enjoyed sending her photographs of the East Study and descriptions of the layout there. Of course, she was dead and no effective retaliation from him to her was possible, but taking the pictures and listing any new stuff, such as a flagrantly surplus nest of mahogany tables, gave him an authentic, malicious pleasure. Sometimes the letters and photographs would come back to the return address he'd put on the back of the envelope, and sometimes they disappeared, presumably thrown away by the people now in the house. He liked to imagine them, perhaps angered beyond by the continuing flow of mail for her, opening the envelope in protest and reading the furniture inventory and enjoying the back-up photographs of, say, a bookcase, hatstand, pouffe.

That kind of unintended, random contact with people whom he didn't know delighted Tane. It gave him the same sort of thrill as television. Watching programmes, he often felt a kind of link between him and performers on the screen. He had the conviction that if one of those professional broadcasters stepped out into the East Study, as the actor does in that Woody Allen film, *The Purple Rose Of Cairo*, he/she would warm to all the homely clutter and excess. This was a lived-in room not some poky, inhospitable cubicle for picking babe names.

He liked to make love to Ursula on the mauvish settee while the television was on a couple of metres away. It was part of that longing for a link with the great outside and elsewhere. He had bought the mauve suite because of its long settee. He was six foot four inches tall. The settee had to provide a suitable and safe site. He'd read somewhere that Eva Braun, Hitler's mistress, used to have a good giggle when distinguished visitors came and sat on a sofa that only recently she and Adolf had used for romance. Tane felt the same when they had guests and some of them took places on the convenient settee.

Ursula had unzipped his trousers and eased her hand inside. Tane said, 'Yes, Lawford might have lost touch with the actual. He was hallucinating? Think of Macbeth seeing the ghost of Banquo just after Macbeth has had him murdered. Lawford believes that if he can beat the witch into silence he'll have some peace. Perhaps he sees the witch as Satan. The trio do come across as evil in the play, don't they?'

The TV news finished and a food programme built around some smirking, amiable chef began. Tane reckoned that a lot of TV shows were obviously constructed to encourage a special sense of intimacy. In many of them, the people taking part worked damn hard to make themselves really likeable. They charmed via the camera. This was how they got to be on the screen at all. They'd have undergone tests in likeability and were then let loose to practise their happy flair in transmission. Programmes that broadsheet critics would label rubbish often had this special matiness and geniality towards the viewer. Tane loved *Top Of The Pops* for instance, presented by that ever-smiling, brilliantly chirpy Jimmy Savile.

Television brought life to Vic and also took him into life. He hadn't ever got that sensation from his time with the classics at Oxford. There was even less chance of it happening now. Who the fuck cared about Apollo wandering around the world looking for somewhere to leave his oracle? No wonder the nymph of the spring at Telphusa tells him to scram and take it to Pytho. He saw staff and students, of course, but felt this was a very enclosed corner.

Ursula had been quiet for a little while concentrating on intelligent finger movements. 'Chote hallucinating?' she said now. 'But does he realize that witches can be vengeful if badly treated? There's one in the play who's so enraged because a woman munching chestnuts tells her to aroint – meaning sod off – when the witch asks her for one that she's going to take it out on the woman's husband who's over Aleppo way. Distance no object, see, when it comes to payback from a witch?'

Vic said, 'There might be some special, transcendental link between witches and chestnuts. Shakespeare knew a lot about that kind of folklore thing. If the witches foresee disaster they've got it right for Macbeth, haven't they, and that's what scares Lawford into antic action?' He paused, knowing that what he intended saying next might be dangerous. 'I feel a kind of shame, Ursula, having watched the awfulness, the deranged, tormented behaviour of Chote in that clip.'

'Shame? How so?'

'Am I one of the causes?'

'Causes of what?'

'Have I helped drive him crazy?'

'Of course you're not and of course you haven't,' she snarled. 'He's done it solo, and gloried in doing it solo. You just happen to be there at the other end of the city. You've done nothing to damage him. In fact some would say you've been insipidly docile. Your only fault is no fault at all – you just happen to be there.'

'Being there is what I mean. By being there I scare him. Whitehall might look on me as a possible top man in a merger. Has this pushed him towards mental breakdown?'

'Oh, stop being so fucking noble and selfless, Vic.' She pulled her hand back. 'This is a kind of grandiosity: you imagine you're so influential.'

'While he's engaged in that idiocy with the sheathed sword and the upset cauldron, I'm calm and safe on another float, surrounded by imported, here-today-gone-tomorrow figures who ensure I get lots of lovely attention and reflected prestige. There's something disgusting about it, something shoddy and sly. Yes, shame, I'm ashamed, Urs. I feel like going over to Sedge in the morning and telling Lawford we should consider proposing the two institutions must join, he the Number One, me his deputy. He's older and I could move up when he retires. He was probably thinking of that kind of change when he came prospecting in the Volvo with the witch. I think the idea would be very acceptable to him.'

'Of course it bloody would. But if you do anything like that you can say goodbye to me, Vic. Or you won't have time to say goodbye, I'll be gone. Screw your courage to the sticking place and we'll do OK out of this crisis. I'm a lawyer and I'm trained to win. I wouldn't want to be linked with some soft-centred, infirm-of-purpose prat who's too decent and limp to grab a chance when it's offered on a plate. All hail Victor Horace Tane! That has to be our battle slogan.'

'You remind me of someone when you talk like this and with those kinds of words,' Tane replied. 'You know how much I hate quotations.'

'They're not from *Hamlet*.'

TWENTY-NINE

1987

Probably because Neddy Lane-Hinkerton almost always came over as such an amiable, good-humoured type, Geraldine must have told him to do the introductory bit at this Preparatory Parameters Survey (U) meeting. Mart could see and understand that a friendly tone, at least as starters to such a difficult conference, was vital. It could be a softening-up tactic. But, also, a university, more than any other brand of institution, ought surely to offer a decent show of tolerance, politeness and civility. Geraldine would probably feel it only proper to abide by some sort of token respect for that kind of pious thinking. Neddy wore a pale green summer-weight jacket, a bow tie, one wing purple, the other yellow with silver stars, and scarlet trousers, also summer weight. His shoes were costly looking black lace-ups; Mart thought Neddy appeared relaxed, unreproachful, light-hearted.

Getting unhurried, joyous stress on to each key word, and speaking from the decidedly left side of his mouth, Ned told Chote, 'On the train, Principal, Geraldine and I realized we both revelled in the chance to get away from London, and come to spend an all too short a time, but welcome, nonetheless, in this gorgeous part of the country where Sedge lies.' He lingered especially on the two different 'g' sounds in 'gorgeous'. There was a nice rhythm to the whole statement. Ned might look flashy in his gear, but he knew how to manage a complicated sentence.

'Yes, Sedge fits in to its good surrounds very well,' Chote said.

To Mart, this seemed sweet and banal enough, yet he thought he detected some Lawford-style arson there, too.

'Oh, certainly,' Geraldine said, with a sort of congratulatory smile, *her* sort of congratulatory smile, meaning it might or might not be truly congratulatory.

'That bastard Dunning deserved what he got, and he knows it,' Chote replied. 'I wish I could have done more. Bruises suit him.' It sounded as though he were answering a reproach, though none had been made. There was no forerunner. He would choose the agenda and decide what came first.

'You mean the incident on the lorry?' Geraldine said. 'We heard something of that – a moment or two of it on television news.'

'They networked it – regarding it as *so* funny and quaint,' Chote said.

'Oh, I wouldn't say that, Principal,' Ned replied.

'Wouldn't you, wouldn't you?' Chote barked.

'When you tell us he deserved it, what exactly do you mean, Lawford?' Geraldine said.

'Did he go to the police?' Chote said. 'No, he didn't. The police went to him, though, and he sent them away, said he didn't want to make any charges. The police themselves told me this. They'd asked him about what you call the *incident* and he'd said it was all part of the Bounty Week show, with me as Macbeth, the great warrior, acting as great warriors did in those ancient times, wielding their sword. The police said there were still red marks on his neck and the side of his face, and probably on the clothed parts of his body, but he insisted these were all according to the scenario and for the sake of authenticity in the *Macbeth* sketch. The sergeant termed it "virtual reality" and commented that we'd both taken our roles excellently in the interests of charity.'

'But that's not really what the onslaught was about?' Geraldine asked.

'Of course it's not what it was about,' Chote said. He spoke crisply, like one who lived among great spiritual and visionary matters and who knew very few others capable of such insights. His pallor seemed to intensify, as though he wanted to assure people that he felt no red rage at Geraldine's need to ask her superfluous question. Mart thought Lawford probably did feel the red rage, but he wouldn't want his skin suffused and mottled at this point. 'It was about something profound, something of massive significance,' Chote said. 'This is what I'm getting at when I say he deserved the beating. He's ashamed, and rightly ashamed, about how he provoked it. We should note what Lane-Hinkerton said during his intro.'

'Which part of what I said, Principal?' Neddy asked.

'The way Sedge has made itself an integral part of this city, part of its, as it were, fine context,' Chote said.

'Well, yes indeed, I definitely stand by that,' Neddy said with slow earnestness.

'And I definitely agree,' Geraldine said.

'Jasper Dunning had questioned Sedge's position,' Chote said.

'In what particulars, Principal?' Neddy asked.

'This would be at our conversation near the cauldron,' Chote replied. 'He spoke as though Sedge would soon be no part of that context, that pleasant local background, because there would be no Sedge.'

Mart saw Neddy glance at Geraldine. They both stayed brilliantly deadpan but Martin guessed they were at Sedge to pronounce pretty much the same thing. 'That's absurd, Lawford,' Geraldine said. 'Sedge will endure.'

'Dunning said this likely extinction resulted from my policies as principal,' Chote replied. 'He's an archaeologist and accustomed to looking for evidence of what brought certain organisations and systems down.'

'I can assuredly understand better why you would have attacked the subversive sod,' Neddy said.

'Thank you,' Chote said.

'It's a blatant, cruel insult,' Neddy said.

'It is, it is,' Geraldine said. Mart waited for her to add

something like, 'And yet, and yet,' but for the moment she kept that locked away. This was still only the opening minutes of the P.P. Survey (U). Pleasantries had temporary charge.

Chote, though, did speak. 'Oh, yes, you two see it as a blatant, cruel insult, don't you, but correct, just the same? It's why you're here.'

Soft-voiced and reeking of reasonableness, Geraldine said, 'But that's such a negative manner of looking at things, Lawford, not at all like your usual forthright, confident self.' Mart interpreted this as: 'your usual blunt, arrogant, bullying self.'

In Chote's office suite, they were sitting with coffees around one end of the conference area's long oak table, nobody at the head in the bigger, heavier, boss-man's chair. Mart knew Chote would find it not just unnecessary but pathetic to advertise his suzerainty by taking this spot. They were on his territory, still his territory, and anyone should be able to sense that immediately without a prompt from furniture. Those who couldn't ought to be sent on a course in sensitivity. As to Geraldine's word, 'negative', he would have regarded it as hopelessly negative to show lack of faith in his own inborn and instant, deep impressiveness.

Geraldine said, 'We – and I speak not just as Ned and myself, but also the minister – we see nothing at Sedge that cannot be put right.'

'Put right?' Chote replied. 'This means you see something, some *things,* wrong. It's as I said – you agree with Jasper Dunning.'

'Yes, can be put right,' Geraldine said. She was obviously used to ignoring what she didn't want to hear, and sticking to her line. 'Yes, can be put right,' she repeated.

'Nothing, but nothing, is in an irreversible state,' Ned declared. If Geraldine could say something twice, he would, too.

'Well, we are glad of that,' Chote said. Mart noticed that 'we' parodying Geraldine's. Mart assumed it meant Lawford and himself. Chote obviously thought of the meeting as two camps, Sedge's insiders, Sedge's malevolent incursers. Mart wasn't sure what he felt about that. Often these days at Sedge he wasn't sure what he felt about a clearly important issue except that it was clearly important. He'd begun to sympathize with that betwixt-and-between, but-on-the-other-hand, character, Sir Thomas More, in Robert Bolt's play, *A Man For All Seasons.*

'You're here about the banquet, aren't you?' Chote said.

'The banquet is inevitably part of it, yes,' Geraldine said.

'And the banquet is one of those things that you would like to "put right",' Chote said.

'We believe that discussion about the banquet could be useful,' Neddy said.

'You think plans for the banquet are not . . . what was your term? Not "irreversible",' Chote said.

'The banquet is a minor issue when seen against the general Sedge debts schedule as revealed in the recent audit,' Geraldine replied.

Chote said, 'But the banquet has become a . . . what's the word, Martin?'

'A touchstone, a symbol or emblem,' Mart said.

'Exactly,' Chote said.

'We feel – that's the minister, as well as Ned and myself – that the banquet should be abandoned,' Geraldine said. 'We advise this with great reluctance. And, of course, we see the difficulties. The invitations will have gone out long ago and the number of acceptances is known and provisionally planned for. But perhaps *very* provisionally. The audit's alarming discoveries were, naturally, private, but rumours about Sedge's financial state have been in the air for a long while. Ned heard some of them when on his earlier visit. The management at Standfast might well have heard them, too.' She struck her forehead with the base of her thumb. 'But, of course, of course, they've heard them. These are smart business people who run a successful company, not the sort to miss crucial whispers and hints. Lawford, we see an alarming danger that *they,* not Sedge, might cancel the booking, out of fear the cost will be unmet. And I have to tell you that such fear is very reasonable. No, I don't have to tell you because you've probably thought it for yourself already – and have decided you'll gamble on Standfast not pulling the plug.

'Have you thought what the result would be if your bet turned out wrong? This would be very damaging publicity – bad not just for Sedge and yourself, but for universities generally, throughout the UK. The higher education sector would look paupered. Now, you might reply that if the cancellation came from Sedge, and not from the Standfast Fort management the publicity would be bad, also. But at least a cancellation by you and Sedge would show that you have wisely, honestly, dutifully identified the problem and willed its solution, not had that solution arbitrarily imposed by others. This is existentialism on the job, Lawford – the acceptance that things are as they are, and acceptance also of personal responsibility to do something about them. I'm sure you'll be thinking of that de Vigny poem, *La Mort du Loup* (Death of the Wolf).'

'Will I?' Chote said. 'Thanks for letting me know.'

Geraldine quoted: '"Gémir, pleurer, prier est également lâche.

Fais énergiquement ta longue et lourde tâche

Dans la voie où le sort à voulu t'appeler.

Puis, après, comme moi, souffre et meurs sans parler."'

Geraldine continued, 'Happily, of course, we're not dealing with death in your case, Lawford, but it's the qualities of the wolf's response that I think could match yours, I'll translate: "Groaning, weeping, praying are all equally cowardly. Get on energetically with your long-lasting and heavy task, in the path that fate has called you to. Then, afterwards, like myself, suffer and die without a word."'

'"Without a word",' Neddy said. 'This was before those "It's good to talk" ads by the telephone firm. And before the "let it all hang out" philosophy.'

'People would see merit as well as defeat in that decision,' Geraldine said. 'They would recognize this resolute behaviour as typical of Lawford Chote.'

'What's the euphemistic military term for what they are proposing, Mart?' Chote replied.

'Strategic withdrawal,' Mart said. This *mot justing* for Chote seemed to be his only role. He didn't mind that. '"Live to fight another day".'

'Except there wouldn't be one,' Lawford said. 'I don't think I'm exaggerating when I say it takes a while for centenary functions to come round again. Mart can tell us exactly.'

The jocoseness was infantile but Mart played along: 'I think it's every hundred years,' Martin said. 'That's the usual way with centenaries.'

'See?' Chote asked Geraldine and Lane-Hinkerton.

Yes, Martin deduced that his only part in this P.P. Survey (U) confab was going to be as a stand-by dictionary and phrase-maker for Chote. Mart wouldn't even get a mention in the minutes, because of (U). As well as feeling a resemblance to slippery Thomas More, Mart also saw a similarity between himself and Nicholas Jenkins, narrator of Anthony Powell's *A Dance To The Music Of Time* novels. He too is more an observer of others than a participant.

'We have pride at Sedge,' Chote said.

'Certainly, you have, and very justifiably,' Geraldine replied. 'And that pride was clearly demonstrated in the centenary concert at the d'Brindle Hall, where you performed on the cymbals yourself. I wish I could have been present. We received several very fine reports of the occasion.'

Mart reckoned she would be late thirties; she was tallish, narrow-faced but not beaky, with very dark hair cut into jagged stooks, smoky blue eyes, nicely rounded chin, good teeth. She had on an amber cotton jacket with wide lapels over a cerise, high-necked blouse, white, slim-cut trousers, black silver-buckled shoes with middling high heels. She wore a thick-band wedding ring.

'Our feeling is that the concert was an appropriately distinguished function to celebrate Sedge's birthday,' she said. 'We understand that the musicians – your fellow players on the night – remain entirely confident that they will, in due course, get paid.'

And so, Martin thought, the meeting moves into its brutal stage – the agonising contrast between Sedge pride and Sedge bankruptcy made explicit, and made explicit without much subtlety or compassion.

'They'll get their money,' Chote said.

'Yes, they will,' Geraldine said, 'if you can accept the proposals, the very constructive proposals, we – that's Ned and myself, on behalf of the minister – the proposals we bring to the survey (U) today.' Lawford had accidentally given her the cue for listing the demands they brought. She had a small, grey canvas travelling bag with her, acting as a briefcase. Geraldine produced some papers and shuffled them to the right page.

'The proposals, then: they are that, with your permission – and, as matters stand for the present nothing can happen without your permission—'

'Your permission is regarded as not merely desirable but obligatory, Principal,' Neddy said.

'Yes, that with your permission a recovery team of eight or nine people will take over the running of Sedge's finances and general admin for a set period of three months and put right what palpably needs to be put right. That would include the payment from special Ministry funding, of the fees and expenses claims of the concert orchestra, including, of course, the fee of the star cymbalist! The concert will be treated as entirely in keeping with the Sedge celebrations and therefore worthy of exceptional, one-off, concert-designated support. Although the team are mainly financial experts they can appreciate and respond to the larger, wider aspects.

'You'll probably say, Lawford, and quite reasonably say, that, on the face of it, at least, there's an absurdity about bringing in this team, with all the extra costs involved – travel, hotel bed and board – when their task is to reduce and eventually eliminate debt. But those costs will run into thousands only, whereas the team will have as its objective the saving of millions. Its members would be salaried by us, of course. Some of your finance and administrative people could be stood off temporarily and continue to draw their pay from Sedge – a kind of suspension, with no implication of criminal or incompetent behaviour. "An organisational re-jigging", that's how the moves could be described. The team might require one or two of your people to stay on to answer any queries and speed matters up by explaining on the spot how the various offices have been functioning.'

Mart thought she'd already have a statistically documented view on 'how the various offices have been functioning'. Catastrophically. The audit said so. But she wouldn't pre-judge anything further. Or not aloud, anyway.

Lawford stroked his long, deceptively sacramental face with the plump, short fingers of his right hand. 'So, what do we make of it, Mart?' His voice was warm with fellow-feeling.

Oh, God, this went further than providing lexicon help, Chote was asking for commitment. 'Make of what, Lawford?' Martin said.

'Geraldine's existentialist proposal.'

'I don't think I've ever understood the proper meaning of existentialist,' Mart replied.

'To put it another way, then: Geraldine and Lane-Hinkerton would like me to vote for my personal extinction *"sans parler"* like the wolf,' Chote said. '"Kindly get lost, Lawford, and keep your mouth shut about the circumstances."'

'I don't think that's at all fair, Lawford,' Geraldine said. 'In fact, it's fucking ungrateful and perverse.'

'They move their holy "team" in for a strictly measured period of three months,' Chote said. 'But, once they're in and, after those three months, Whitehall decides this is not quite an adequate period to work the required miracles, how are they to be got out? Geraldine and Lane-Hinkerton dodge off again from the boredom and rush of London, poor dears, and they arrive to announce that the squad needs another three, or six or twenty-six or sixty-six months.

'And, Mart, there's another issue. The takeover group will establish their own pattern of running things during those three months or more. That's why they would be here, isn't it? The team's own pattern of running things will be deemed successful, or at least promising by the minister, Geraldine and Lane-Hinkerton. They would have a career interest in declaring it good, and they'll see one major consequence of this. The new style of management will most likely be very different from the previous style of management, meaning mine. They will believe – they will choose to believe – that I could never adapt to the changed, splendid system and should therefore be force-fed early retirement, eased out, kicked out, replaced.'

'This is a totally distorted version of things, Lawford,' Geraldine said. 'We are here to help you.'

'That so?' Lawford replied.

'Our aim is to prevent development of a situation where all funding to Sedge stops. I mean the most basic, regular funding. You'll probably not be able to pay staff or keep the lights on.'

'As to "*sans parler*", Principal, I would say that, on the contrary, there has, in fact, been a great deal of discussion, not "*sans parler*" in the least,' Lane-Hinkerton stated.

'What we've had is a long diktat from Geraldine and we don't like it, do we, Martin?' Chote replied. 'Geraldine, you say you need my permission to move in your gifted, encroaching platoon. We do not give it. We refuse them entry, do we not, Mart? I'm applying my existentialist right and duty to take responsibility for my unique selfhood.'

Mart thought Chote might be taking responsibility not just for *his* own unique existentialist selfhood but for Mart's also, and Mart didn't really care for this.

THIRTY

2014

Mart reckoned he must have done the chairing job of the statues committee pretty well because there was unanimous agreement that he should pose as both Lawford Chote and Victor Tane, or Victor Tane and Lawford Chote, when they all moved out into the grounds of the Sedge and Charter campuses, or the Charter and Sedge campuses, to select and test possible sites for the statues. They moved between the two campuses in a convoy of seven cars like some head of state arriving at a conference with his administrative and security back-up.

The group's all-round approval showed Martin that he had been right from the start to avoid commitment and partisanship; and, particularly, to resist any invitation to inner-circle croneydom from Lawford Chote. Mart saw that the committee trusted him, and he felt grateful. Even when they were considering what might be the most suitable ground for the mooted double statue on a single plinth they wanted Mart to represent both Lawford Chote and Victor Tane, or Victor Tane and Lawford Chote. Logistically, this involved shifting just short of a metre from his position as, say, Lawford, to the other end of the imagined plinth where he would become Victor, or vice versa.

Members accepted that there were hints in what people had said during the several indoor meetings which might indicate a special affection or a special hostility towards one or other of the pair and that this could result in favouritism when picking what were regarded as the best site or sites and who should occupy it or them. Mart thought of that unpleasant tiff between Jed Laver (Industrial Relations) and Gordon Upp (Linguistics) because Upp thought Laver had denigrated Lawford Chote and protected Tane.

Martin recalled that there had been a lot of profound discussion in committee sessions about the feet of the two statues if the ultimate choice was for the double statue on the single plinth, rather than an individual plinth for each. Someone had very perceptively pointed out that the feet were not really feet at all according to the normal definition of feet, but only part of the same stone entity as the rest of the statues. Martin went along with this analysis and felt it would be stupid to pretend he had to free his feet at one end of the plinth – e.g., the Lawford end – in order to move and become Victor Tane at the other end, or to free his feet at the Victor Tane end and become Lawford Chote. Instead, Martin believed he should step fluently and easily across the gap and turn into a stone Victor Tane, if he had been a stone Lawford Chote up until this point, or around the other way. The possible double occupancy of a plinth did make some difficulties but Mart thought common sense could deal with them. The committee – and Martin himself – should surely keep in mind continuously that the statues and their feet and footwear were, when one came down to it, all from the same chunk of stone or brass. The feet and their shoes did not stand on the plinth in the usual meaning of the word 'stand'. The feet and shoes were *of* that plinth, not *on* it.

As to height, at five foot ten inches Martin came somewhere between Chote and Tane, or Tane and Chote, but this did not trouble the committee. They could supply the plus or minus inches in their imaginations, a plus if Mart was Tane and a minus if Chote. After all, when the actual statues rather than

Mart were in place, people looking at them would have to make a much bigger imaginative jump than was required to see Mart as someone taller (Tane) or shorter (Chote). They would have to see stone or brass as living flesh, bone and blood – quite a step. In the kind of university teaching of English Literature that Mart did there was a theory summed up in the phrase 'The author is dead.' This didn't necessarily mean the author was dead, although, obviously, many of the writers studied *were* in fact dead. But what the phrase signified as a piece of critical theory was, once the author published his/her work he/she had no further control of it. The reader was supreme and could make of the item whatever he/she liked. She/he could say, 'I love this poem because when I first read it I'd just had one of the best liver and bacon dinners ever.' This might seem irrelevant to many, but it is not irrelevant to that particular reader. Similarly, the matter of Mart's height or lack of it could be adjusted to the correct measurements in the imaginations of the committee.

Using what was known as 'The Method' style of acting, Mart tried to think his way into the very differing minds of each principal and convey their personal qualities by the way he held his head as he gazed forward on his notional plinth, and his styles of stance. When he was Lawford he set his face to show general belligerence, some contempt for most of humanity, but also a determination to give as many components of that humanity as he could the boon of higher education. It wasn't easy to get this mix of curmudgeon and philanthropist. Mart attempted it by shaping his lips as for an imminent foul-mouthed snarl, arranging his shoulders as though to help with the delivery of a concussing left fist punch, yet softening his eyes into a gaze proclaiming not just goodwill to all men, but super goodwill to all men, and women.

For Tane, Martin went for a look of quiet orderliness and decency but coupled with a resolve to see himself on top in the long run. This was largely a chin matter. Mart didn't make it jut like a reckless challenge but he endowed it with four-square solidity and strength. Also Mart put one of his feet slightly forward of the other signifying the likelihood of a sudden, unexpected dash to victory, despite seeming until then only a runner-up to Lawford and Sedge. This potential spurt forward was akin to, but not the same as, the move Mart made when changing ends of the double occupied solo plinth.

Undergraduates on their way to and from lectures of course noticed the cluster of women and men at the various selected sites on the two campuses staring at Mart in one of his transfigurations and judging its suitability as against other nominated sites.

'What's it about?' a girl asked. She had on short purple shorts, a detached stiff white shirt collar fastened around her neck by a stud, but no shirt, only a black singlet, and a denim waistcoat. She carried a laptop and a half full water bottle.

'It's about the future,' Elvira said. 'But in the past.'

'What future?' she said.

'You,' Elvira replied.

'Me? How?'

'This is Lawford Chote,' Elvira said.

'Lawford who?' the girl replied.

'He had you in mind.'

'How could he? He doesn't know me. I'd remember if I'd met someone called Lawford. And Chote.'

'We're talking about 1987,' Elvira said.

'1987? I wasn't born then,' the girl replied.

'That's why I said he had you in mind. You were the future.'

'So the future is now, is it?'

'It was then,' Elvira said.

'Then? But this is not 1987 and he's here. You're all gawping at him. He's the present, not the future nor the past.'

'These are merely technical points,' Elvira said.

'The course I'm on is technical,' the girl said. 'I.T. Information Technology. There's nothing mere about it.'

'He'd be pleased to hear you argue back like that.'

'Well, I can tell him, can't I?' She yelled at Mart, 'Hey, Lawford or whatever. I'm technical.'

Mart liked the look of the purple shorts and wished he could have smiled in appreciation. But this would have been wrong for his present embattled Chote self.

THIRTY-ONE

1987

Martin had another phone call from Neddy Lane-Hinton. 'As I believe I said, Mart, a little while ago, I have what could, I think, be reasonably termed a special extra mural relationship with Geraldine.'

'Yes, you did mention something along those lines.'

'It puts me in a particularly influential position vis-à-vis her.'

'Yes, I can see it might.'

'A screwing arrangement as simply that – a screwing arrangement – would surely strike both Geraldine and myself as slightly, or more than slightly, degrading. Animal-like.'

'Yes, I understand.'

'Well, you would, you would, Mart. We've heard how you've made yourself something of a specialist in that general area as mentored by *Lady Chatterly's Lover*. But Geraldine and I talk. There is mind-contact as well as bodily. I don't say one is superior. They can comfortably co-exist, not at all like Marvell's *A Dialogue Between The Soul And The Body* where each is sniping at and thuggishly berating the other. The soul calls the body a dungeon and the body calls the soul a tyrant. Foolish polarisation. Ger and I avoid that.'

'This happy acceptance of the two modes I can understand, too.'

'In one sense, of course, she is a boss figure.'

'She's the sort who'll probably qualify for a damehood in due course.'

'Possibly. I don't think I've ever had it off with a baroness. I'm very keen on that gear they wear in the Upper House.'

'She might let you try it on,' Mart said.

'So, at any rate, there are times when our conversation is complete and utter business, and therefore in the nature of orders, instructions, to me, the tone and message unaffected by our extra, unofficial and personal connection. That's as you would expect. But occasional topics arise which, although clearly business items, can also be influenced in some measure by that sweeter, fleshly link we've established.

'For instance, Mart, Geraldine versus Chote in the barren (U) meeting that never took place. She was altogether serious when she told him that if he didn't accede to the proposed takeover of Sedge management by a Ministry team she would cut off all funding to him and Sedge so there would be no money for basics, including wages. She could probably find in the articles of British university governance a ruling to be implemented by someone of Geraldine's rank, that if the behaviour of a principal, president, provost or chancellor became flagrantly chaotic and damaging, there would be not only an option to stop further waste of taxpayers' money, but a directive to do so, an absolute duty.'

'Yes, there is an impression of power about her,' Mart said.

'There is power, but there is also a tenderness, something which I can occasionally reach mainly on account of the exceptional closeness we achieve from time to time outside the parameters of usual university polity. For instance, Mart, the Sedge wages.'

'I get no word from the bank that mine have been discontinued.'

'Nor will you, Mart. Not so far, anyway. Why am I so sure?'

'Yes, why, Neddy?'

'I intervened.'

'In what sense?' Mart replied.

'I made an appeal to that tenderness I mentioned just now, and which I knew was present, though not immediately detectable.'

'You have a special "in" with her?'

'Yes, it could be put like that, I suppose. When a stopper on Sedge funding was first considered as leverage against Lawford Chote I naturally thought of that delightful as it were bonding lunch at The Lock Gate. Although you took something other than the black-pudding hash, I felt a real and rare harmony existed between us immediately.'

'Certainly,' Mart said. 'I meant no disparagement of the black-pudding hash. It was just that my taste buds on that day, and specifically and limited to that day, required something different.'

'There's no accounting for taste buds. The occasion remains in my memory as a brilliantly pleasant one, and, consequently, I found I could not go along with Geraldine's plan to activate a general curse on Sedge. I tried to envisage the impact of the sudden block put on your pay. It would not be simply a matter of withheld money. No, such withholding indicates a unilateral destruction of contracts. It is uncivilized. It is anti-civilized. The foundations of good order are shaken, perhaps terminally shaken. This is not the kind of pain one wants imposed on a good friend with whom one has, so to speak, broken bread. I described my reaction to Ger. She knew, of course, that we had made such a fine occasion of that visit to you. I said I didn't wish to be a party to such undeserved punishment of someone I had come to think of as a chum – and I hope I'm not presuming, Mart.'

'Not at all,' Mart said. 'A feeling shared.'

'Thank you, thank you,' Neddy replied. 'Many a boss would grow angry and dismissive to have his/her plans brazenly resisted in such outright fashion by a subordinate. But this is where that tenderness aspect began to tell. She could look sympathetically on the kind of sound relationship established by you and me at The Lock Gate. Why? Because, Mart, she knows from our own – hers and mine – relationship that I am one who prizes such strong and warm affection between two people. I don't mean she thinks there's a gay element linking you and me. No. But she can appreciate the worth of simple, heartfelt camaraderie and companionship. She and I have that, though boosted by occasional vivid, intemperate sex. The sex is fine but not essential, Mart.'

'I think I follow, Ned.'

'She listened to my objection and for a while grew silent, obviously weighing its worth. Her head was on my chest and I could trace the twirls and ridges of her left ear via my skin. As a matter of fact we were just winding down after a very charming love passage on a Turkish rug in the sitting room of her exceptionally stylish home in Highgate, London. Her husband was on a fishing trip in Scotland and their son away at Eton. As you probably know, even a top-quality rug can scorch knees during this kind of vigorous set-to, but Geraldine had, has, a conscience about taking me into any of the beds there. I could appreciate such nice delicacy and still do, Mart. To invite a man to follow her up the stairs surely indicates calculated intent, whereas to yield to sudden, ungovernable desire on an imported, beautifully handwoven floor covering gives a touch of inevitability and *jeux d'esprit* adultery. Of course, unless she's on top *her* knees don't suffer. But that's simply one of the privileges of high office.'

'Adaptability is a splendid quality,' Mart replied.

'I think I mentioned previously the biting.'

'Yes. You spoke of its controlled nature.'

'There was none this time, controlled or uncontrolled.'

'Did you deduce something from this, Neddy, like the dog that didn't bark in the Sherlock Holmes story, this silence giving the great detective an important clue?'

'Her mind, preoccupied to a degree. Do you remember what was said about President of the U.S.A. Gerald Ford – that he couldn't chew gum and think at the same time?'

'Gerald and Geraldine similar?'

'She had some thinking to do, yes, after what I'd said. She seemed to feel it would be inappropriate – sort of tapas behaviour – to nibble at my neck skin and/or nipples, given the circs.'

'Well, yes, there has to be a protocol about that kind of thing,' Mart replied.

'My body was naturally confused. It is used to a certain sequence and the biting figured in it as a major component. She raised her head off my chest and I thought she was about to get back on track with the tooth work. Not at all. Although we were on a damned expensive Turkish rug and had been drinking some decent brut champagne she was plainly unsettled, Mart. Moving up a little so that her breasts rested reassuringly on mine she said that OK, she would accept my line about the potential pay freeze, and its impact indiscriminately on all Sedge staff, you included. Instead, she would closely focus her reaction to where she could now see it should have been focussed from the outset.

'Geraldine thanked me for helping her to think more clearly

and equitably. She detailed a new plan. Possibly through Rowena Chote, who was more likely than Lawford to appreciate the realities of their situation, Geraldine would offer Lawford a U.F.C. package that would compel him to take early retirement, early meaning immediate. This could be managed without too much humiliation for Chote and little loss of dignity. She said the Sedge debts were only a part of the trouble, though the major part. She couldn't ignore reports of that Macbeth idiocy on the charity float, and the soaked spectators. Nor did she like the rumours about staff quitting Sedge and unease among Sedge students as to the worth of their degrees – if, that is, Sedge was able to continue courses and award degrees. So, Victor Tane would be appointed at once to a joint principalship of the two merged universities and would host the Standfast Fort Banquet backed by further moneys from the U.F.C. She says merger she says.

'I realized, Mart, that although she hadn't got her teeth into me she had into Lawford Chote, regardless of what she'd said about only minor humiliation and loss of dignity. She stood and retrieved the champagne cork. I said I'd get rid of it and the bottle in a public waste bin on the way home. She said, "Good" and came and snuggled down again with me on the rug in front of the imitation coal gas fire on at full blaze to prevent the absence of clothes leading to a chill. Anyone looking in would have regarded this as a very homely tableau. "I'm glad all that's tidied, Ned," she said.'

'I expect she was,' Mart said.

THIRTY-TWO

1987

But Martin loathed some parts of Geraldine's revised campaign, especially her plan to drag Rowena into the crisis. Geraldine would ask for her help in convincing Lawford that he should chuck the Sedge principalship immediately and disappear, pension and severance lump sum gorgeously intact, though not his reputation. Ever since he brought Rowena out of her booze-aided snooze at his inaugural, Mart had felt a strong, subliminal link with her. They had chimed. This was big. He wanted her well-being, her lifelong well-being. He didn't think Geraldine's 'tidying' scheme would secure that. He had to protect Rowena. Theirs was a unique, mystical connection established by *Lady Chatterly's Lover,* and Mart's commentary on its sex theme. Rowena depended on him, even though she didn't know it. He owed her. He had words that could rout her gin coma.

There were two possible outcomes if she did what Geraldine required. Neither was good for Rowena and/or her marriage. If she succeeded and Lawford eventually agreed to cave in, he would always, in his eminently paranoid way, think he had been pressured, betrayed, by a traitor. Hadn't Mart seen that kind of crazy, elaborate suspicion take hold of him on the day of the Volvo reconnaissance to Charter Mill? Such mistrust could permanently put a shadow over his relationship with Rowena. Alternatively, if he rejected Rowena's advice and refused to leave, his notion that she belonged to a conspiracy against him could be even more powerful. He would see her for ever as a turncoat. And when by some other means Geraldine got him out of his job he might still regard Rowena as one of the gang against him and not want her in his life any longer.

Mart went back to that phrase, 'by some other means'. He did accept now that Lawford could not stay much longer in the principalship. Neddy had told of Geraldine's switch of tactics against Chote and accounted for it by describing her essential, inner tenderness towards Mart himself and all the rest of the Sedge staff. Maybe. But what Martin gathered from the phone chat with Lane-Hinkton was that if one scheme for getting rid of Lawford had to be abandoned, she would find another: she'd give up the idea of cutting off Sedge's money, but she'd trawl for some substitute way of making him go – Rowena's pleas perhaps. Geraldine's 'tenderness' rested on an adamantine backup. Perhaps, too, she had an Education Minister driving her to fix an end for Lawford, regardless of how. Mart, for so long chary, even afraid, of commitment now knew he had to get committed. He must tell Lawford direct, with no involvement of Rowena, that he could not win in this battle with Geraldine and Whitehall. He should agree to what sounded like excellent terms from Geraldine and move, with little publicity and embarrassment, into an enjoyable and peaceful retirement. Rowena would bear no taint of treachery. Mart thought he'd give Lawford a ring on the internal phone and try to fix an appointment. Most probably, Chote would be shocked and possibly hurt to get such a recommendation from him. This Mart regretted. Perhaps he, not Rowena, would be regarded by Lawf as the rat. Up till today Chote had seemed to value Mart's opinion on all topics. Now, that esteem would inevitably be withdrawn. Never mind. Martin sought only the best for Rowena and Lawford – particularly Rowena – and had come to believe that the best was for both of them to bow out.

Mart's intention to ring for an appointment turned out to be unnecessary, because it was Chote who arranged the get-together. Mart was giving a lecture to undergraduates on what he called 'The Destruction Of Language For The Sake of Meaning' in some Shakespeare sonnets such as: 'When my love swears that she is made of truth/I do believe her, though I know she lies.'

He thought he heard a door open behind him and realized that most of the students were looking at something to his right. Mart stopped his commentary on the word 'believe' in the sonnet – which meant its opposite – and turned his head to see what the disturbance was. Lawford Chote stood a few metres away. He came forward to the lectern. 'Please allow me to interrupt for a moment, would you, Professor Moss?'

'Of course, Principal,' Mart said. Of course, of course.

'Something has happened which I need advice on, not simply from you, Professor, but from a representative sample of Sedge students, such as your class here today. By a striking coincidence the theme of your lecture has a bearing on what I wish to discuss.' He edged Mart away from the lectern and stood behind it. Mart went to sit in the front row of the hall.

'Recently, a meeting took place in Sedge which did not take place, just as in the poem he believes his mistress but doesn't. It couldn't have taken place because you, Professor Moss, were present and this makes the existence of the meeting impossible.'

'Yes, I had that outlined for me,' Mart said.

Chote was in shirtsleeves. He had on the waistcoat, but not the jacket, of a grey suit, with a gold watch chain across half his midriff. The shirt was white with narrow crimson stripes. It was open-necked, with no tie. What looked like a couple of inches of cream thermal vest showed behind it. His face radiated combativeness as it often did, but Mart also saw there a lurking sadness, even despair. Perhaps that was to be expected, though Mart wouldn't have expected it from *him.*

Chote said, 'At this meeting which didn't take place there was a discussion which didn't take place, either, as Professor Moss could explain to you all if the meeting and discussion had occurred.'

'Certainly,' Mart said.

'One of the points that couldn't have been made at this non-meeting was a warning from a Ministry of Education official that if I did not give up my principalship of Sedge at once all funding to the university would cease. We would be put into a state of siege. Obviously, this would have been worrying if the threat had been voiced. I would have rejected it and subsequently decided to ask a typical Sedge group – say, Professor Moss's class and Professor Moss himself, whether I would have done the right thing in dismissing that proposal and threat with maximum, principal-style disdain.'

'Disdain is the only possible response,' Samantha Colley, a red-haired girl at the end of a row, said. 'Oxford showed it to Thatcher. We have a precedent.' Sandra had been in one of his seminar groups last year.

'Could I call for a vote: Stay or Go?' Lawford said.

Every student in the room raised a hand for Stay.

'Thank you,' Chote said.

'But the professor didn't vote,' the girl said.

'I think he should go,' Mart said.

THIRTY-THREE

1987

Among the student attack group that broke commando-style into the centenary banquet at Standfast Fort's mahogany panelled, high-windowed, historic Plain Parlour, Mart spotted a few of his own English Literature undergraduates, including Sandra Colley, the red-haired girl, today wearing a turquoise jogging outfit and almost matching green mountaineering boots. Mart wondered if they'd had cooperation from someone in the Parlour work force – a cook, a waiter, a sommelier. This, after all, was a fortress and built to keep enemies out. Had someone deliberately left a door unlocked? But why? Perhaps there were Sedge students doing part-time jobs in the kitchen or around the tables and sympathetic to the Lawford cause, grateful for his expansionism that had given them a university place.

The timing of the inrush struck Mart as suspiciously perfect. They entered, yelling and baying, a few minutes into a speech by Victor Tane as newly appointed principal of the combined institutions of Sedge and Charter Mill, following the well-earned retirement of Principal Chote from Sedge.

It would have been kindly, Mart thought, if they could have left two empty chairs at the top table for Rowena and Lawford. Had they been invited? Was there a forwarding address for them? Judging by what Martin knew of Tane, such an invitation seemed the sort of decent, commiserating gesture he might have made. After all, they were a legitimate, renowned part of Sedge's centenary; in some ways more legitimate and renowned than the Tanes. It occurred to Mart that in the future there might be a proposal for some sort of memorial to honour Lawford; say, a statue. If so, a complementary or counter proposal would probably emerge: another statue, but this one, Victor Tane. The duality would almost certainly lead to endless debate about which statue should get the more prominent site; would the Tane statue dominate if the two were close because of his height; would it be necessary to shift the statues around the city so that each had a spell in the Charter campus and a spell in the Sedge; would it be mere sentimentality to give Chote a statue although he'd sunk Sedge in its previous form? But if a plan for two statues went ahead would they be on a shared plinth or each have his own? Mart had a feeling that the plinth allocation question would entail profound, lengthy disputation. Although some might regard plinths as neutral, uncontroversial slabs, Mart suspected they could become of towering significance then.

Of course, the Chotes would not have accepted an invitation to the Plain Parlour banquet. Lawford would imagine Tane was crowing over him, lording it and being magnanimous in victory. Lawford would probably phrase it as 'being sodding magnanimous in victory the gaping-nostrilled, Latin versifying prat', though.

There were fourteen or fifteen in the assault party, Mart reckoned, nine men, five or six women. They came in four units of four, four, three, three or four. That could mean they'd been smuggled in by instalment as opportunities appeared. It took about two minutes for them to assemble at the far end of the Parlour. Mart thought he could detect clever tactical organisation, like troops in street fighting advancing in small formations, maximising cover. Many of the diners failed to notice the build-up, their attention on Tane's vacuous celebratory words. At first, before things went destructive and dangerous, the students seemed satisfied to stand at the far end of the Parlour and shout and wave cardboard banners with 'Bring Back Lawford', 'Lawford's The Lad', 'Lawford We Love You' in crimson letters. 'Hail to Lawford', they shouted. 'We want Lawford'.

'Tane, get back to your fucking Mill,' Sandra Colley screamed. The lettered message on her banner read: 'Chote IS Sedge, and Sedge is Chote', like Rod Steiger as Napoleon in the film, *Waterloo*: 'I am France and France is me'. 'Foul Betrayal', another banner mourned and another said: 'Down with the Thatcher Lapdogs'.

Apart from a pause or two and a few sentences that didn't

quite add up to good sense, Tane bravely kept going. At the end, there was unfervent but respectful applause. Then, while they waited for the desserts and toasts, Tane, at the top table with the minister, the Lord Mayor and Lady Mayoress, Ursula Tane, editor Alan Norton-Hord and other persons of interest, seemed to fall into vigorous conversation, possibly about the grand prospects for the new double-unit Sedge. Somehow, Tane seemed even stringier in formal garb. The polarities of black jacket and bow tie on a white shirt appeared too definite and strong for his wispy frame. But he had doggedness and, for a moment, Martin thought that by ignoring the bellows and snarls, he might have triumphed. The banners were lowered suddenly and chucked aside.

Martin soon saw why, though: the protesters wanted their hands free to snatch missiles from the feast remnants and, crockery, cutlery, glass on the guest tables. These opening salvoes were reasonably harmless items – fruit, various types of cheese, leftover slices of sticky toffee pudding, and gateaux, bread rolls. The targets were all on the top table. Again Mart sensed a battle briefing pre the offensive, its objective clearly stated. Geraldine, in an elegant navy blue boardroom suit was hit by a half orange on her lapel. Something wettish and murky lodged itself in Tane's scarce hair. Ursula got half a ripe Camembert under her right eye and clawed the bits off and hurled them back, hissing, 'I'll kill the rioting jerk.'

Despite Roy Gormand's forecast that Mart would be on the top table, he was, in fact, seated in the body of the hall at a very ordinary spot and remained untroubled.

Standfast had security staff, male and female, and several of them came into the Parlour at a rush now and moved fast towards the invaders. This was when the missiles became more dangerous as some serious fighting began as security tried to drive the students out. Crockery, cutlery, glass and even chairs were hurled. A china tureen shattered on the flagged floor when half a dozen wrestling guards and intruders barged against it. Several diners, some of the students and some of the security posse, were cut about face and head, and Sandra fell, concussed by a flying chair. Someone phoned for the police and ambulance service.

After about half an hour the Parlour was in something like working order again. Sandra recovered, the rest of the intruders were cleared from the big, handsome room, some possibly arrested, some possibly treated by paramedics from the ambulances. Tane, still with whatever it was darkening his hair, resumed his speech, saying that some birth pangs were unavoidable during the creation of the changed institution and that the 'little recent unfortunate turmoil was, in fact, a heartening sign of vigorous life'.

THIRTY-FOUR

2014

'"**D**ear Professor Moss".'
    Mart read aloud to the statues committee a handwritten letter he'd received from Rowena Chote apparently living now in Hastings on the south coast. She'd obviously decided in view of what was coming to say that she should shun the familiarity of his first name.

> Word has reached me here of a proposal to erect a statue of my late husband, Lawford Chote, at Sedge University. Information is sometimes slow in arriving to this area and I hope I am not too late to declare in the strongest terms that the proposal should be rejected outright. Lawford would detest the idea. He was devastated when, Professor Moss, you announced that you thought he should step down at once from his post as principal. He regarded this as incontrovertible evidence of his defeat. He laid great store on your opinion in any controversy following the happy incident at your inaugural lecture upon being promoted to a professorship. Lawford would maintain, if still alive, that vanquished leaders should not be commemorated in any form. He'd consider such a seeming accolade as meaningless and grossly hypocritical. He would find it

especially obnoxious, Professor Moss, that you, after your base defection, should now have the unholy impertinence to chair a committee whose ostensible purpose is to decide the form of a monument to him.

Whatever his faults might have been – and there certainly were some – Lawford believed in absolute honesty in all aspects of his life. He was made of truth. He would want no statue, of himself. I, similarly, do not want it and abhor the suggestion. May I ask you, please, to do all you can to get this fart-arseing fucking idea negated. I address my appeal to you because you were the one who brought him down and therefore should be aware of the notion's absurdity more than anyone else, though I'm not sure you *are* aware of it or ever will be.

Yours faithfully, R. Chote.

'Blimey,' Elvira said.

'What incident at your inaugural, Mart?' Lucy said.

'So we go for Tane only, do we?' Gordon Upp said.

'Do we?' Mart replied.

Lightning Source UK Ltd.
Milton Keynes UK
UKOW05f1019200617

303713UK00001B/42/P